The Calling

Elaina Harper

Published by Saint Nilo Press

Library of Congress Cataloging-In-Publication Data

Contact: Elainaharper2024@gmail.com

ISBN: 979-8-9909544-0-3 Print, Paperback
ISBN: 979-8-9909544-1-0 Digital, E-book

Cover Design by Karen Lewis, Simply Amusing Designs

First Edition: August 2024

Dedication

For My Only, the father of my children and my biggest cheerleader. Thank you for letting me pursue my dreams.

The Calling

Chapter One

The Confession

The third-worst day of Paul Wainwright's life started with a phone call at 3:13 a.m.

"Father, a riot broke out earlier. Now I've got Marvin Foster and James Armetta holding hostages in the kitchen. Foster is asking for you." Raul Martinez, the associate deputy warden at the Ballentine Correctional Facility, let the words tumble out of his mouth.

Paul felt the blood leave his limbs. "Me? Why?"

"No idea. Warden Shackleford and a hotshot team of so-called experts have been negotiating for hours without any progress. We've got suits from Houston chatting them up, offering them all sorts of shitty promises—no offense. They aren't biting.

"The warden is considering storming the kitchen, but he doesn't want all of this to turn to shit. Again, sorry. Election year. It won't affect him directly, but why give some politician some reason to piss and moan about prison reform?" Paul fumbled in the nightstand, finding his glasses, while throwing out a loud yawn that Martinez ignored. "Then, about ten minutes ago, Foster asked for you, won't give an explanation. We can't figure it out. Have you worked with him before?"

"I can't imagine what—"

Martinez cut in. "This is their only demand. You don't have to come, and I know it's a lot to ask. But it isn't like you have to meet with them in person, just talk to them through our internal phone system. I don't know what to expect if you come. But this was their request, so I'm relaying the message. Maybe it will end it for us or . . ." He let it hang.

Paul balanced his phone on his shoulder while adjusting his glasses as he processed Martinez's words.

"Father, you there?"

"I'm here." He shifted to the edge of the bed, letting his feet hit the floor. "Tell them I'll come. However, they have to release the hostages. Unharmed."

Martinez snorted. "I'll tell them, but I can't guarantee it'll do any good."

***

"The fight started after dinner. Witnesses say Armetta was barking at one of the guards. He was offended about some thing or another. Then Foster jumped in. Some say Foster was defending Armetta. Others said he was trying to stop him from losing his head," Warden Shackleford said, briefing Paul as they sped through the prison's administrative wing. "The guards tried to break it up. It went sideways. Now I've got six prisoners, including Foster and Armetta, and three guards barricaded in the kitchen."

"Weapons?" Paul asked.

"The guards have tasers and pepper spray." Shackleford's pace increased. "We keep firearms locked in a cabinet in the guard station in case a riot breaks out. Then the guards have access . . ." He swore. "Our guys didn't have time to arm themselves."

Martinez jumped in. "It's likely Armetta and Foster have homemade weapons. Knives. Shanks. Not that they'd need them. You've seen the size of Armetta. The man could throw a tank across a room."

"Which means Foster could lift a 747," Paul mumbled.

Shackleford pointed toward his office. "I'll let you talk to the operations team. Then we'll put you in contact with Foster and Armetta." He balled his fists. "Look, I just want this to end."

Paul stopped short at the warden's door. He pointed at Martinez. "I told you I'd talk with them once they released the hostages unharmed."

"Like I said, Father, they wouldn't agree to that." Martinez shrugged. Exasperation crossed Shackleford's face.

Paul squared his shoulders. "Fine. Where's the phone? I'll tell them myself."

***

Twenty minutes later, after winding through several buildings in the sprawling prison complex, Paul waited in the multipurpose room in front of the kitchen's green doors. The last-minute coaching by the negotiation team had already fleeted from his short-term memory and was replaced with prayer and panic.

"Look, you can back out. I didn't expect them to meet with you in person," Shackleford explained, as they listened to the jumble of men's voices combined with noises of heavy objects being moved behind the doors. "We can rush them."

Glancing at the officers donned in full tactical gear, Paul replied with false confidence, "I gave my word."

Martinez inhaled. "When you talked to them in the warden's office, it wasn't part of the deal. You sure? These guys are monsters."

"I'm aware," Paul said in a faint whisper.

Foster and Armetta's behaviors weren't surprising. As gang leaders, they left the remains of trouble in their wake. Paul's lungs seized thinking about how nothing made him question his life choices more than spending his Thursday afternoon prison ministry with Ballentine Correctional's two most disruptive prisoners. On his drive back to Saint Daniel's every week, he'd take his time returning to the rectory, chatting with God, asking for guidance while wondering, *again*, if maybe he'd chosen the wrong life path. Now, listening to the sounds abate behind the metal doors, he wondered if that same life path might lead to his end as soon as he walked into the kitchen.

An unnerving creak caught him by surprise as one of the metal doors opened, revealing a shadowy expanse. Four inmates stepped through the darkened void as if they'd just exited a black hole. The prisoners nodded to Paul.

"You crazy, Father," one muttered as he shuffled past.

"You coming in or what?" hollered Armetta from somewhere in the depths of the kitchen.

"Where's the guards?" he called through the crack in the door. "I said *everyone*."

"No can do," Armetta shot back.

"Then I can't, either." Paul crossed his arms, discreetly wiping the sweat from his palms onto the sides of his shirt.

The kitchen door stood partly open. Shackleford hitched his thumb toward the kitchen, indicating someone should walk through the doorway. The riot team began marching.

Paul held out his hand. "No."

"Listen to Father Wainwright!" Martinez ordered. Everyone stilled.

"Marvin! James!" Paul took a tentative step toward the kitchen. "There's a crew out here prepared to take you down. They've got guns drawn and they're ready for business. If you want me to come in, release the guards. If you don't, it's the other guys."

Low sounds came from the dark expanse. Armetta shouted, "We'll give you one guard in exchange for the priest. Take it or leave it."

Shackleford whispered, "What do you want to do, Father? Not too late to back out."

"What's the odds of everyone coming out alive if those guys go in?" Paul asked, pointing at the tactical crew.

"If there's a fight, Foster and Armetta could be dead within seconds. Depending upon the condition of the guards, who knows? They could already be dead," Shackleford said.

"The prisoners seemed fine when they came out," Paul replied.

"A ruse." Martinez shrugged. "Probably went along for the fun."

"What'll it be?" Armetta's voice boomed.

"Bring out one of the guards and I'll come in."

"It'll be a few," Armetta responded.

"You have two minutes," Shackleford challenged.

"Fuck you!" Armetta barked.

More bumping and moaning came from the darkness as well as the dull inaudible undercurrent of conversation between Foster and Armetta. The kitchen doors opened a fraction more. An overpowering stench of blood and feces wafted through, announcing the presence of a wheeled metal table, now shoved into the multipurpose room. Another odor followed, reminding Paul of something woody, yet acrid.

"Smells like they used an entire can of pepper spray," Martinez mumbled, looking down at the battered guard on top of the table.

A team of medics swarmed the guard. Paul steadied himself while he looked at the horror lying in front of him. Stepping in the direction of the man's feet, he gave the guard a blessing, taking his time, not only to ask God for deliverance and healing but to stall what might be a similar fate for himself.

"Hey, Priest! You coming or what?"

Before Paul stepped into the darkness, he looked over his shoulder at Martinez and Shackleford. "Pray for me," he said.

A light from down the hallway gave off enough illumination for Paul to make out sizable debris lying on the floor. Standing for a beat, he let his eyes adjust.

Armetta hissed, "Shut the fucking door."

Paul obeyed, listening to the ominous creak and hoping for a better outcome than the guard he'd left outside. With the kitchen sealed off from the multipurpose room, a bulk of a man stepped out of the shadows. His dreadlocks suggested images like snakes sprouting from Medusa's head. He hefted a crate in front of the entrance, then began fortifying the space with portable tables, boxes, and food supplies.

"Give me a hand with this." He pointed to the remaining containers covering the floor. Paul lugged a case of powdered eggs toward the man. Armetta snatched it, filling in a hole in his blockade. "Get those other ones off the floor."

"This way," he said, once he declared the space secured. Armetta waved his mammoth hand in the direction of the light.

The sound of footsteps made an eerie hollow noise as they walked along the hall. "How are you holding up, James?"

Armetta stopped in mid-step and eyed him. His low voice came from inside his chest, causing a chill to run through Paul. "Foster asked for you. Not me."

"Yes, but how are *you* doing? I mean, do you need anything I can tell the warden about when I go back out?"

"You funny," Armetta scoffed, walking through the doorway where the light had originated. He announced, "God showed up. You happy now?"

Paul scanned the cluttered room. Shelves stacked with food cans and cleaning supplies lined the walls. The space reminded him in size of the all-purpose closet, which doubled as his office. Unlike his office, two unconscious, bloody lumps lay in the corner with their spent taser guns discarded off to one side.

Foster rose from a seat made from stacks of industrial-sized cans of green beans. He shifted one of the top cans to the ground as he stepped to Paul. The can bounced once with a hollow clang and stopped at the man's feet, as if it resigned itself to the same fate as the guards. "Thanks for coming, Father. I mean it." He stuck out his beefy hand.

"They alive?" Paul asked, hoping his voice hadn't come out like a croak. He tilted his head toward the guards while shaking the man's hand.

"Yeah." Foster lowered his head. "Sorry about that—really am."

Paul began to kneel, ready to bless the guards, and then changed his mind. Despite a master's degree in clinical psychology and another in theology, as well as the hasty negotiation tactics briefing he'd been given on the way to the prison's kitchen, he recognized how ill-prepared he was for this task. But it didn't take anything more than common sense to know turning his back on Foster and Armetta while praying over the guards might not be in his best interests.

"Before we start, I'll pray."

"No can do." Armetta puffed his chest.

"That's fine, I didn't ask you to," he replied with a fleeting calmness.

Paul raised his hand to his forehead, then lowered it to his chest, and finished crossing himself by touching his left and right shoulders. Before either man could argue, Paul gave a heartfelt prayer, asking for guidance for Foster and Armetta and blessings upon all in the room. He asked for forgiveness for those who had inflicted and been afflicted by any wrongdoings. For good measure, he individually blessed Foster, Armetta, and both guards.

"'Bout time," breathed Armetta.

"You wanted to see me, Marvin?" Paul asked, facing Foster, while keeping one eye on Armetta.

"Yeah, I need your help, Father."

"What can I do?" he asked, sitting on the only box out of arm's reach from either of the men.

Foster nodded toward the door. "Jimbo, take a walk."

"What? You gotta talk *now*? Can't you have your private chit-chat when you're in solitary?"

"Just . . . Five minutes. Okay? Then we'll talk about giving up."

"Please, James, I wouldn't mind some water," Paul said.

Armetta rolled his eyes as he stormed out of the storage room. "Five fuck'n minutes."

"What can I do for you, Marvin?" Paul asked as Armetta slammed the door behind him.

Foster ran his hands across his bald head. He settled onto the green beans, using the errant can to prop his right foot. "I want you to hear my confession."

Praying his voice stayed even, Paul asked, "Are you telling me, in the middle of this riot, you wanted to see me so I could hear your confession?"

"Yeah." Foster leaned forward. "Please?"

He swallowed. "Of course."

Reaching into his pocket, he retrieved his stole. With an unceremonious flick, it unrolled, landing atop one of the empty taser guns. Paul kicked the taser toward the corner.

Foster's eyes grew wide. "They let you in here with that scarf?"

Paul studied the long, satin cloth. He'd grabbed it off his hanger on his way out the door, rolled it, then shoved it into his pocket. Now, he felt foolish for bringing something that could be used against him. "I didn't discuss it with Shackleford or Martinez. My stole is part of my uniform. I use it when I perform my duties."

He assessed Foster. Paul may have been five inches taller, but Foster had at least sixty pounds on him. Placing the stole around his shoulders, he said, "I can see how this could be used as a weapon. So, Marvin . . . don't."

Foster lifted his hands. "We good. Just don't let Jimbo see it." Crossing himself, he said, "Bless me, Father, for I have sinned. Been a long time since I've done this. I got a lot to confess. I've done really bad things. Hurt my mother. You got a mother? You'd never hurt your mother, right?"

"My mother has passed, but let's continue with you."

"Yeah, sorry. My condolences."

"Thank you. Go on."

"Never killed anyone before. Can I be forgiven for that ahead of time?"

Images of the tortured guard laying on the metal table danced through Paul's head as he motioned to the unconscious men lying against the wall next to a pool of blood. "The reality is they need immediate medical assistance. You can save them. We can end this standoff. They don't have to die. Do you feel true remorse, Marvin?"

"Yes, Father. I do. I have reasons. I know it's wrong," he muttered. "I want to save them."

"Taking a life is very serious."

"Yeah. I've had time to reflect. Biggest penance I'll have is I'll probably never get out of here 'cuz of this."

Paul, normally patient with the confession process, knew there were too many variables working against him to have Foster's confession drag out. He inched his eyes at the guards, nervous this could be his own fate. Any second Armetta would return, his mood unpredictable. "Do you have anything else to confess, Marvin?"

Foster laughed. "I'm sure I broke all Ten Commandments. Can I say that and get to the point?"

"If that'll work for you." He asked again, "Anything else specific you would like to confess?"

"I might later. Will God forgive me? I need to make sure I'm square with Him and I have a chance at Heaven. I promised my mother . . . Never killed anyone before."

Paul hurried his ministering, absolving Foster of his sins, and gave him a penance, to which Foster readily agreed. He'd just slipped his stole into his pocket when Armetta burst into the storeroom empty-handed.

Armetta's eyes narrowed, glaring at the men. "What's going on?"

"Just a friendly chit-chat." Foster's hand clamped Paul's shoulder while pointing at Armetta. "We gotta talk. Me and Jimbo. Can you give us a minute?"

Paul glanced at Foster. "I'd rather talk to you about ending this ordeal."

"I know. It's time to give up." Foster's hand stayed glued to Paul's shoulder as he navigated him out of the storage room. "Just a few minutes. Then we're done," he said, shutting the door.

Pacing the dim corridor, Paul heard the muffled sounds from inside the storage room of indistinguishable shouting and objects falling from the shelves. The commotion caused him to wonder if Armetta and Foster were talking? Fighting? Or were they blowing off steam and recklessly destroying the contents of the closet as one last act of rebellion?

With his hand poised over the doorknob, vibrations bounced off the floor from Armetta and Foster's movement. As the noises became concise and deliberate and the cursing became distinguishable, Paul decided he'd wasted enough time. Whipping open the door, he found the men in opposite corners, fire shooting from their eyes.

Foster rushed Armetta, extending his right arm. He placed his fingertips on Paul's chest and in a fluid motion, pushed him back out of the storeroom.

"Stay out of this," Foster warned, kicking the door closed.

Grabbing the doorknob again, Paul found it locked. "Marvin! James! Open up!" He rattled the knob while banging on the door.

When no response came, Paul moved toward the kitchen, ready to clear the blockade. The storeroom door flew open. Foster stood in the doorway, doubled over, panting.

"I'm okay. It's over now."

"What about—"

Foster held up his palm. A sheen of moisture beaded above his brow. "Had to happen, Father. He was bad news. What he did to those guards . . . Sick and wrong." Foster wiped his hands on his orange jumpsuit as he skirted past him into the shadowy kitchen. "Jimbo needs you. Go see him." He gave a quick laugh. Paul flinched. "Thanks for helping me with my salvation too. My mother . . . She'll be happy now.

"Wait! What do you mean? Is James alright?" Paul turned his head toward the quiet storeroom.

He snorted. "Glad you can't talk about that confession."

A sick sensation surrounded Paul, settling into his stomach as he grasped Foster's implication. Praying he misunderstood, he darted into the storeroom.

"James!"

Paul froze mid-step looking at the sight in front of him. Armetta's body lay in a contorted V shape. Blood gushed from his nose and mouth, leading a path to three teeth lying on the concrete nearby. A portion of his dreadlocks splayed across his cheek, like dead snakes flung into a pile. The haunted look in James Armetta's lifeless eyes, staring off into the great beyond, confirmed the inevitable.

Flashbacks of that fateful day fifteen years earlier rushed through Paul as he glanced around the room. His mouth agape as numbness seeped through his limbs. Steadying himself on the doorjamb, suppressed trauma bubbled to the surface threatening to erupt and wreak havoc on the emotions he'd successfully managed to ignore his entire adult life. With more strength than Paul knew he had, he fought—and won—the quick battle, pushing those feelings back to the depths of his subconscious.

Bending to his knee, Paul reached into his pocket a second time for his stole, placing it around his neck. He touched his forehead, then touched his chest and tapped both shoulders before he began praying over the dead man.

In the distance, the sound of thrown boxes echoed into the hall. The noises of the metal door creaked open. And then, Paul heard Marvin Foster announce, "I give up."

Chapter Two

The Demons

Almost one week after the riot, the sting from James Armetta's death landed as fresh as the night Paul witnessed it. Self-loathing voices taunted his waking hours, reminding Paul of his failings. The haunting hollowness of Armetta's brown eyes followed him around every private corner, as the events of the night continued to replay in his consciousness.

Of course, he'd seen death before. He'd even witnessed the unfortunate aftermath of murder. But now he understood Marvin Foster wanted permission with his confession to kill Armetta and absolution as his ticket to Heaven.

If Paul's own self-admonishments and the blow-by-blow replay of last week dancing through his head weren't enough, his community unintentionally stepped in to rub salt in a raw wound. Monday morning, Monsignor Costa announced a surprise lunch for the three priests at the Wagon Wheel, Ballentine's only restaurant. Figuring the monsignor just wanted to dig in further for more dirt from last week's riot, Paul opted to beg off, saying he'd eaten breakfast there hours earlier.

"Not today." Monsignor Costa beamed. "Father Wainwright, you cannot miss this."

Paul cast his eye at his mentor, recognizing Costa's expression. "If you wouldn't mind, Sir—" he started.

"Nonsense." Costa clapped Paul on the shoulder, misreading the rest of his thoughts as humility.

"Join us," Father Morales jumped in. "The pecan pie will be a prelude to Heaven. And if you don't finish your piece, I will be happy to help you out." Paul gave him a dry look. Morales added, "Besides, Monsignor is paying. Let's find out his true agenda."

Out of excuses, and tired of listening to the sound of his own thoughts, Paul found himself at the Wagon Wheel. Between bites at lunch, Monsignor Costa regaled the restaurant patrons with stories of Paul's bravery, though most of the incredible tale came from Costa's imagination. Paul sipped his iced tea, keeping an eye on the time, wondering how long he needed to be present before he reminded everyone it happened to be his afternoon off. He'd already sent a text to his brother before they sat down to eat, announcing he'd be over later that afternoon to hang out.

Once Monsignor grew tired of retelling the fantastic narrative of the riot to the locals, Paul fielded questions, hoping nobody whose relative was locked in Ballentine Correctional sat eavesdropping at a nearby table. He kept his answers tentative, giving the same types of replies he'd already regurgitated, focusing on positive results and God's mercy for the captive prisoners and the guards. However, in the back of his mind, his thoughts gravitated toward his true humiliation: Marvin Foster suckered Paul in the name of God.

Morales elbowed him, taking another bite of his sandwich. His eyes bored into Paul. "Now that you have saved these lives, are you up for a vacation, Father? We all know you've been past due for a week or two off."

Paul couldn't decide which direction to go with this line of questioning. Escaping the constant buzz around Ballentine had an appeal. It was the most excitement the town had since the fire station burned down five years earlier. Additionally, he felt suffocated by the continual pats on the back from Monsignor Costa, who enjoyed the local attention over Saint Daniel's junior pastor's role in ending the prison riot. However, vacations came with their own pitfalls, namely more time to think and relive the past.

"Actually, Father Wainwright," Monsignor Costa started, the edges of his lips ticking upward in a small sign of approval. "Your vacation will have to wait just a little bit longer. But I promise, you will be able to take some time off."

Paul brightened. "That's perfectly fine. With the basketball tournament, the prison ministry, and the work at the Tyler Women's Clinic, I'm staying pretty busy. I didn't have any true plans at this time."

"Good. Good," Costa said. "I received a phone call from the bishop today, and I think you will agree, you are the perfect person for this honor."

"Honor?" Paul asked, hoping he hadn't raised a skeptical eyebrow.

Costa offered a warm smile. "The diocese received a call from James Armetta's family today. Because you were with him in his last moments, they want you to give the eulogy at their son's funeral this week."

Paul felt the air leave his lungs. "Sir, I'm not sure—"

Costa laughed, cutting him off. "I *am* sure, Father. I assured them you would be happy to do so. They are expecting you in Little Rock on Wednesday."

***

"James Tyrone Armetta," Paul began Wednesday afternoon. He looked out at Armetta's mother, inconsolable and bawling as a relative clutched her heaving shoulders. "He was the only son of Olivia." He pointed to the front row as she cried louder.

Most of Paul's consultation with Olivia Armetta came over the phone Monday afternoon as he sat in his office rubbing his temples. Though not Catholic, she'd said Armetta mentioned attending his Thursday ministry in his letters home and how he found it enlightening. In the woman's grief, Paul realized her comment equated to a nostalgic connection between the two of them.

He knew James Armetta showed up only to score future points with the parole board. Armetta and Foster came on a regular basis, bored and looking for a chance to cause chaos. As a source of Paul's frustration, no Bible verse or loving comments about Christ's Peace ever mollified their unruliness during those afternoons. Sometimes, his and Foster's disruption, distraction, and disrespect continued through the worship service until a guard or two barked at them to knock it off.

Using the basics Olivia Armetta shared, while ignoring his own sense of loss and longing, Paul strung together a series of creative platitudes. His eulogy, he hoped, conveyed dignity while giving Armetta's mother a sense of peace. He wanted to spin a tale of forgiveness while making Armetta's impact on the world sound meaningful. Now looking out at the frail and distraught woman, who heard nothing he said, Paul wondered if the effort he'd extended mattered at all.

"I knew James from my prison ministry." Paul pushed his glasses farther onto his face. "He stood out as a leader in the inmate community, commanding respect as he atoned for his mistakes."

Olivia bawled louder. "He was such a good boy," she wailed.

The woman clutching her muttered, "Yes Ma'am. You know it. You always knew it. And this good preacher man knew it. God knows it too. Amen, I say. You raised a good one."

"Amen," Olivia blubbered, wiping her eyes with a fresh tissue. Another round of crying started again, taking over the room.

Paul let the words sink into the smattering of Olivia Armetta's obligated family and friends, feeling these sentiments were a better explanation than anything he could have offered. He let out a breath, which he hoped didn't sound like a sigh. "Our God is forgiving. Loving. He knew James's heart. He knew the circumstances which brought him to his eternal rest."

Paul cringed. He hated clichés like, "eternal rest."

He finished telling stories, all given to him by Olivia Armetta: James as a child, James helping his grandmother, and James winning a blue ribbon for his junior high track team. Paul concluded his eulogy with, "Though we can't understand why God took him before his time . . ." another phrase he hated, ". . . we know, James will always live in our hearts. His lasting impact will be with us long after today."

"Amen," Olivia Armetta sobbed, using the shoulder of the woman next to her as a pillow. "Amen."

Paul's stomach lurched. The only lasting impact James Armetta had on him was the image of the tortured guards who were still battling for their lives.

***

Paul drove back to Ballentine an hour after the funeral, sipping his Coke and hoping to stave off the physical exhaustion competing with his misery. In truth, he was grateful to be away from Olivia Armetta. He had no more stories, true or fiction, to share with the dead man's mother. Worse, though her inquiries were innocent, no matter how many times she asked for some sort of closure, Paul couldn't bring himself to share James Armetta's last moments.

His jaw tightened as memories fluttered in and out of his head, breaking up the monotony of the trip. Guilt mocked him. He let his mind vacillate between two main ideas, wondering *again* how he could truly be cut out for this vocation, and more to the point, if Foster confessed to a different priest the night of the riot, would Armetta still be alive?

It was the confession that plagued Paul the most. As a Catholic priest, the seal of confession made it so he could not discuss Foster's admission with anyone—not in casual conversation, not under threat of imprisonment, and not even under the threat of his own demise. A priest who violated this rule could expect immediate excommunication. He couldn't even speak to authorities about how he now knew Foster planned the entire ordeal, rather than a self-defense ploy Foster's lawyer now professed.

Paul had been afraid of disappointing Monsignor or Father Morales by allowing either of them to hear about his failure the night of the riot. Instead, before the funeral, he'd found a priest in Little Rock to hear his confession. He asked for forgiveness for rushing through Foster's own confession and not taking steps to protect James Armetta's life.

The priest he'd spoken with missed significant aspects of Paul's confession, including how he was a member of the clergy. Instead, after finishing with his Act of Contrition, the priest said, "Do not commit that sin again," giving him two Hail Marys as penance.

Two Hail Marys? What kind of trite penance was this? He'd already recited an entire rosary that morning. If Paul had heard this confession, he'd have at the very least suggested something along the lines of "help another in need." The measly punishment was a stark contrast to the lasting image of James Armetta's mother bawling and clutching her relatives, an image Paul was certain would be forever burned into his memory.

Now, as he drove on the busy Arkansas Interstate, on his way back to Texas, he processed the inevitable. His demons were determined to keep him company on his four-hour drive to Ballentine while all thoughts kept returning to one simple fact: because of James Armetta, Paul's body count increased by one more.

His cell rang. "How you holding up, Paulie?" Allison asked as he connected it to his truck's hands-free device.

"Not you, too," Paul groaned. "Monsignor call you?"

She laughed. "No. But I heard the news. You've been ignoring my texts. I know you negotiated a prison riot last week. I don't care how strong you think you are, that was probably some tough shit you dealt with, Padre." Her voice grew serious. "I'm guessing it brought up some baggage."

"Sorry, I didn't respond before. It was . . ." Paul searched for the word that had been eluding him. "Surreal." As he finished the sentence, it occurred to him that Allison was one of the two people in his life who would assume the ordeal was taxing on multiple levels. "Honestly, it makes me question everything I do. Ally, I was helpless." The words came out as a whisper.

"Well crap, Paul. Have you talked to anyone? You can't keep this in. Who do priests talk to?"

"Their twin sister, generally."

"Most people aren't as lucky as you to have a therapist in the family," Allison pointed out. "But seriously, that's too much trauma. Especially for you."

"I'll get over it," Paul mumbled.

"*You* don't get over it. Still waters, Paulie."

"I appreciate your concern. I'll be fine. Eventually."

"Do you have anything to get your mind off the riot? Is there a basketball tournament coming up?"

"In a few weeks. In fact, this year we are playing for the Tyler Women's Clinic."

"Well, congrats," Allison said. "A charity near and dear to your heart. We'll be there. Refresh my memory. Who won last year? The priests or the seminarians?"

Paul cleared his throat. "The priests. Thank you. First practice was last Friday. Costa bragged to the bishop on Monday that I'm this year's ringer."

"Of course he did! Paulie, you made the Texas All-State team all four years of high school. The University of Arizona recruited you even though you were from a small Catholic high school in nowhere Texas. When does that ever happen? What did they call you back then? A 'basketball phenom'?" Allison's voice grew serious. "You should have gone pro. You're six-six and have been on the clergy team since you were ordained and came to Ballentine. I think everyone could figure it out."

"It gave Costa something to talk about." Paul sighed.

"He thinks of you as his son," Allison said. "He has since . . . well, he always has."

"Honestly, I was at practice last week, but only physically. I'm sure my heart will be in it later. I need a bit of time."

"Damn—sorry. I know you hate it when I say that. You need to give yourself some grace. You of all people. The folks at the prison don't know your past. And unless you became a whole different person in the last fifteen years, I doubt most people know why this hit you so hard."

"Ally, it was more than the riot and the murder of the prisoner. But I can't talk about the rest of it," Paul said, wishing for a loophole in the confession process.

"Well, I'm here if you change your mind. If not me, call Chuck. He's been through this too. You aren't alone. You have both of us. But no matter what, I hope you can find some ways to cope, tools to help you as you go through this." She added, "I'm not discounting God, prayer, reflection. Okay, I am discounting reflection. The last thing you need is to dredge up more memories." She paused. "Look, Paul, maybe it's time to consider letting the prison ministry go. Maybe you've outgrown that season of your life?"

Paul rubbed the bridge of his nose. "Ally, I'm going to stick with the prison ministry."

"You can't bring Mom and Dad back," she interrupted. The emotion was long gone from that statement.

"I'm aware. But maybe I can help someone else find God. And maybe there might be fewer victims."

"And fewer orphans," Allison added. "It would be nice if you could make that happen. I love that about you."

"But you don't believe I can do it."

"No. Not you alone," Allison admitted. "But I believe you believe it. I also believe you need a distraction to clear your head."

After Allison's call, the self-loathing voices began again. The idea of returning to Ballentine, to his dinky office, to the incessant nosy parishioners, and to the prying eyes of Monsignor Costa and Father Morales brought him dread. The more Paul thought about what waited for him at Saint Daniel's, the more he felt his chest constrict.

"I could use a distraction, God," Paul grumbled, as he drummed his fingers on his steering wheel.

As if on cue, the car directly in front of him slammed on the brakes, shattering his admonishments.

Scanning the horizon, he registered the sudden bumper-to-bumper traffic crawling on Interstate 30. Picking up his phone, while keeping one eye on the road, he opened his traffic app reading about the 18-wheeler pileup near Texarkana. "Forty-five-minute delay. Not the kind of distraction I had in mind," he grumbled.

The nagging in the back of his head reminded him of his calling—his duty—to stay in the traffic jam, just in case he could minister to anyone up ahead who might be hurt. Paul allowed those cautionary voices to mingle with the chastising demons who were still chiding him about Armetta's death. Tired of listening to all of it, Paul opted for a new route, with the hopes of leaving his demons on the Interstate. The next exit, less than a mile away, promised coffee, bathrooms, and a detour through Shreveport, Louisiana, which was now the easiest way back to Ballentine.

Chapter Three

The Distraction

As he drove on Louisiana's Highway 3, the first signs of civilization—a Dollar General, a boat storage lot, and a deer processing plant—suggested Paul couldn't be too far from the outskirts of Shreveport. Rolling down his truck window as he entered a small town, mindful of the speed limit drop, he let his senses absorb the springtime late afternoon, smelling the sweet aftermath of what must have been the residual of an earlier rain. Random smatterings of yellow and white jonquils, pleasant byproducts of April in the South, popped through the grass on the sides of the roadway, breaking the monotony of the drive.

Paul fiddled with his radio, searching for an NBA game to interrupt the silence in his cab. "Mavs game should be starting . . ." He looked at his dashboard clock, sighing. "In thirty more minutes."

A quick burst of light momentarily blinded him, causing Paul to tighten his grip on the steering wheel with one hand while throwing his other in front of his face. Squinting, he scanned the horizon, catching sight of a disabled green Honda on the shoulder, one side of the car visibly lower than the other. Paul shielded his eyes again as the sun's reflection off the car's side mirror deflected for the second time into the truck's cab.

A distraction! "Thank you, Lord."

A tall brunette stood in the gravel on the side of the road in an animated phone conversation, as Paul pulled onto the shoulder behind the Honda. The woman sandwiched her cell between her head and the red shoulder of her suit jacket, using her arms to emphasize her point. He caught parts of sentences. "Tow truck . . ." "You could . . . you know . . ." and after a momentary silence, the brunette scowled. With her lips flat, she barked, "Thanks for nothing!"

Ending the call, the woman groaned while stomping her foot. Her heel landed sideways on the pavement, causing her to trip. She toppled to the ground with her matching skirt riding up to show more than Paul expected. He looked away, giving the brunette time to compose herself. Instead, she raised her fists to Heaven, oblivious to the oncoming cars and what he saw moving in the tall grass behind her.

He called through his passenger window. "Excuse me." The woman looked in his direction. Paul pointed. "There's a snake."

"Holy shit!" she screeched, scrambling to her feet.

The woman threw the phone in the snake's general direction while high-stepping backward toward Paul's truck. The creature slithered away, the swaying grass being the only reminder it remained nearby.

"Thanks," she said, gasping for air while clutching her chest. "I hate those things. Did you see what kind?"

"No. But it was tan and fat." He pointed to the woman's car. "Can I change the tire for you?"

The brunette inched closer to the cab's passenger window. "Appreciate the offer but I don't have a spare. I'm waiting for a tow truck." She pointed toward her phone, lying where it landed near the tall grass. "Tow truck driver told me it's gonna be at least ninety minutes." The woman raised her hands. "Today of all days. I'm already late for work."

"I could give you a ride," he offered.

With a soft Southern drawl, which didn't match the skepticism plastered on her face, she said, "Sweet of you, but I've seen too many horror movies. Don't misunderstand me, you seem like a nice guy. Honest-looking—a choir boy—as my mama would say." She wiggled her fingers toward the grass. "Even saved me from that beast."

Paul processed the words. A woman taking a ride from a strange man? He looked down at his slacks and button-down Oxford. His priest vestments were packed in his suitcase. Nothing he wore suggested he was a man of the cloth.

The last bits of light peeked through the high clouds, giving the ground an amber glow. A strong sense of chivalry refused to permit him to leave the woman stranded on the side of the road. Perhaps the next driver who came along would not have the purest of motives.

Paul asked, "Why don't I retrieve your phone? I'm guessing you don't want to go into the grass." The expression on her face suggested she hadn't made up her mind. Raising his hands, he amended, "Tell you what. I'll put your cell on your trunk. That way there's no misunderstanding of my intentions. Will that make you comfortable?"

The woman bobbed her shoulders, which Paul decided meant he had permission. Walking on the side of the road, with an eye out for the snake, he scooped up the remains of her phone, placing it on the Honda's trunk.

Crouching, he examined the tire. "It's completely shredded. You'll need a new one."

Paul caught the surprising smell of vanilla. He drew in another breath. Turning, he saw the brunette next to him, realizing the sweet aroma must be her perfume. As he inhaled again, a slight smile escaped.

She stomped in a circle on the asphalt, throwing her hands up in frustration. "This day just gets better and better."

He offered a silent prayer for a resolution to her situation.

"You mentioned you're late for work. I can certainly understand not wanting to get into a car with a stranger. I'm sorry I suggested such a thing. I wouldn't want my sister—"

"Don't worry about it." She waved her hand. "It's my problem. Just . . . well, you caught me at a bad moment."

It seemed obvious to Paul this was the kind of penance he should have been given for his transgressions with Armetta. Helping another in need. God provided this distraction.

"How about if I call an Uber for you? And I'll wait for the tow truck. Will that be okay?"

The woman didn't mask her surprise. "Why would you do that?" she drawled. "I mean, that's nice and all, but why?"

Paul shrugged. "I'd like to do something."

She gestured toward the grass. "You saved me from the snake. Thank you. I'll be fine. I can wait in my car. I'll just call work."

He motioned toward the trunk. "Your screen's shattered."

In one fluid movement, the woman closed the lids over her soft brown eyes while clenching her jaw. The pose made her seem more like a sculpture than alive. Paul noticed her cheekbones, high. Her lips, red. Her nose, slightly upturned. Even in her disheveled state, her natural beauty shone through, while her feminine actions spoke in a language of their own. The woman appeared swift and strong, yet delicate and vulnerable. In a quick moment of selfish prayer, Paul thanked God for this perfection.

Thoughts he hadn't entertained in years invaded his head. Paul pushed them out with equal speed. She glanced in his direction. Those same thoughts flooded back in. This time they lingered with no promise of leaving.

The brunette grabbed her phone and examined the broken pieces. She opened her mouth and then closed it again.

Raising an eyebrow, she asked, "You wouldn't mind calling an Uber? Don't misunderstand me. I'll cover the fare. And you'd wait here for the tow truck? Can I pay you for your time? I mean, I'm already late but I don't want to be much later."

"I'd rather you help out the next person you see in a troublesome situation," Paul countered.

"Thank you. I mean it. Today has been . . . Well, let's just say this flat tire was probably the best part." She shook her head. "No, your kindness has been the best part."

Paul opened his mouth, ready to tell the woman his vocation required him to help others. His actions weren't truly "kindness" but just an aspect of his calling. As a Roman Catholic priest, he was required to willingly do God's will, no matter what was asked. Instead, "Happy to help," tumbled out.

***

Friday morning, Paul scanned his office while tapping his pencil on his desk. The scratch paper in front of him held a few notes, which would need to be transformed into something inspiring before Sunday's Mass.

He released a loud sigh, embarrassed he held resentment for being trapped in such a small space.

His dinky office was the large closet at Saint Daniel's, once a catch-all of rickety plastic shelving holding office supplies overflow church staples as well as mops and brooms. Since Paul joined the parish, the mops and brooms had been relegated to the rectory, and the only excess floor space now held his desk, chair, and bookshelf. It wasn't the cramped quarters he minded, though with his lanky frame he had zero room to stretch his legs, as much as the lack of a window and the garish avocado-green walls.

Even with the absence of sunlight, the biggest issue with Paul's workspace was its proximity to Monsignor Costa's and Father Morales's private offices. Both men had exceptional hearing and too much time on their hands. Small matters, such as what book was on Paul's desk, what podcast he was listening to (even when he wore earphones), and who he was emailing were often reasons for the two other priests to pop in, making inconsequential inquiries or micromanaging his duties, as if after seven years on the job, Paul was unfamiliar with his responsibilities. The continual oversight wasn't out of distrust, but instead it was because the two men had nothing better to do in an East Texas city of 9,000 where less than 10 percent of the population was Catholic. The local culture thrived on gossip. Costa and Morales were doing their part to fit in.

While Paul focused on composing his sermon, the ring on his cell interrupted his task. He frowned, knowing any private communication would be considered breaking news to his colleagues. Putting aside the notes for his sermon, he eyed his phone. He didn't know anyone in Louisiana.

Declining the call, he glanced across the hall at Monsignor's office. Costa looked up, raising an eyebrow. Paul gave a shrug and turned his focus back to his immediate task. The phone rang again with the same number.

In the corner of his eye, he saw Costa rise from his desk. The old priest hovered more than normal lately, another byproduct of the prison riot. So far, Costa used the stand-in-the-corner approach of smothering instead of asking for a detailed account of the previous week's events. Paul didn't want to think about Armetta's death any more than he wanted Costa to treat him like a grieving child. Deciding the strange call was a better alternative than a potential meet-Jesus talk with Monsignor Costa, he answered.

"Paul Wainwright." He winced, realizing he had forgotten his title.

"Hi, Paul?"

At the sound of her voice, an involuntary smile flashed across his face. Everything, including the depressing green walls and Monsignor Costa's hovering eyes, suddenly looked better. Paul stood, ready to bolt out of Costa's and Morales's earshot, but instead, the force of his chair rolling behind him and hitting the shelves caused three boxes of Saint Daniel's envelopes to crash to the floor.

"Good morning," he said, balancing his cell on his shoulder while kneeling and scooping envelopes back into the boxes. "This sounds like the woman I met a couple of days ago who was having a bad day. I see you have a new phone."

"It's Delia, please," she said with a lilt in her voice. Paul envisioned her slender wrist batting the air, punctuating her words. "Your number was on the receipt for the tire. I wasn't expecting you to buy it, that was a total surprise. I'd like to send you a check."

"Not necessary. Remember, I said you could help someone else."

She laughed. "We were talking about the Uber ride. I'm serious. May I have your address? I don't like to be obligated."

"Can we call it even?"

"I'll tell you what. If you won't let me pay you for the tire, can I do something? I mean, I think I kind of owe you."

"You don't owe me. Please. But . . ." Paul closed his eyes as he remembered Delia's perfect face. Unexpected and surprising thoughts percolated from the recesses of his brain. He shook his head, erasing the ideas and refocusing his efforts on cleaning up the mess on the floor.

He crammed the envelope boxes back onto the shelf and turned in time to see Costa halfway across the hall, ambling in his direction. Perhaps the company of someone who didn't know about the prison riot might be a welcome break. A quick lunch? A chance to talk with Delia about Christ's sacrifice? What could it hurt? Find a soul to save while taking a break from the oppressive air of the past week? In addition, he could find some way to serve in Shreveport at the same time as extra penance for Armetta's life.

Paul shoved the tentative cautious suggestions back into the depths of his head. Under normal circumstances, he would never consider lunch with a strange woman. The appearance of impropriety alone! Plus, Shreveport was seventy miles away. *But this once,* he reasoned. It was the perfect distraction from the madness of the past week.

The words spilled out easier than he expected. "Next Monday, I'll be in Shreveport—that's where you are? I could meet you for lunch. I have some business there."

Leaning over his desk, he scribbled, *call the Shreveport Diocese/hospitals/shelter/nursing homes,* on his calendar to remind him to drum up some anticipated "business."

Delia's voice softened. "I'd like that. Wait? You don't live in Shreveport?"

"No. I'm in Ballentine, Texas. About an hour and a half away. Nobody's heard of the town unless you have relatives in prison. But I . . ."

On cue, Monsignor Costa knocked on the doorjamb of Paul's office. Momentarily startled by such a polite interruption instead of his normal abrupt eavesdropping, Paul held up a finger. When the old priest didn't budge, he mouthed, "I'll get back to you."

Costa nodded, cemented in the doorway. Paul frowned, knowing any of his calls could go on for two seconds or two hours and the monsignor would still have waited.

Paul paced the scant space behind his desk. He said to Delia, "Let's shoot for Monday. This is your number. Right? I'll get in touch with you on Sunday to confirm. Would that be okay?"

After saying their goodbyes, Paul stared at his shoes, waiting for his face to steady. As he raised his head, he caught Costa's watchful expression.

"How can I help you, Sir?"

"Good to see you smiling, Father. Your sister?"

"No. Actually, it was the woman I told you about who was stranded on the side of the road. She called to thank me." Paul turned up his hands, hoping it was enough of an explanation.

"I trust you took the money for the tire out of our charity fund. If you haven't, please do so."

Paul nodded to humor the old man. However, he had no intention of being reimbursed.

Costa stepped into his office. "Also, I know you've had a taxing week." The monsignor softened his face. "If you need time off . . ."

"I'm fine, Sir."

"If you want to take a vacation . . ." He raised his palms. "Perhaps get away and clear your head?"

Paul straightened his shoulders. Though Monsignor expressed the best of intentions, the events from last week were still too fresh. Being alone with his past would do more harm than good. "I appreciate the offer. But I'd rather work. Is there anything else?"

"Yes, actually. I need you to fill in for me at noon Mass today. I have a few matters to handle at the hospital."

"Sure. Happy to help." Paul reached across his desk to the bookshelf above. He selected his book on homilies, thumbing through for a ready-made one for such short notice.

"Thank you, Father Wainwright," Costa said, but didn't leave.

Paul pretended to read a selected passage, while aware Costa's eyes stayed on him. Swallowing, he ensured his collar wasn't too tight. When Monsignor didn't take the hint, Paul looked up. "If you don't need anything else, Sir, I'll need to prepare for Mass."

As he heard Monsignor's footsteps move down the hallway, Paul perched on his desk, crossing his ankles. He scanned the day's Gospel reading, recognizing the very act of staying busy brought him peace, allowing him to focus his thoughts on something other than Armetta's lifeless face. Ditching the pre-written sermon, Paul turned his Bible to Philippians. "But one thing I do: forgetting what lies behind and straining forward to what lies ahead." He laughed. "If it were that easy."

However, Paul noticed as he stayed preoccupied while the weekend wore on, his thoughts strayed away from the prison riot. Basketball practice Friday night turned into tacos and beer with his fellow teammates. Saturday morning, he counseled at the Tyler Women's Clinic and met up with his basketball teammates at the park for a few pickup games with the locals. The energy he poured into his activities kept his demons at bay, strengthening his sense of purpose.

Complimentary feedback from parishioners of his message at Sunday's Mass continued to boost Paul's spirits. It also gave him a bit of confidence to text Delia, confirming lunch plans. When her reply came back, he'd been talking with Monsignor and Father Morales, who were in the middle of a cribbage game. Paul knew they saw the smile cross his face as he glanced at his phone.

"Your sister?" Morales asked, an eyebrow arched.

"You know," Paul rose, rocking back on his heels, "that reminds me. Excuse me. I should give Allison a call."

Monday morning, Paul hummed as he entered the common area wearing a clean pair of khakis and a dark green golf shirt. Father Morales sat at the kitchen table, playing on his phone, and sipping his coffee.

"Morning, Father," Paul said, jingling his keys.

"Morning to you too, Father," Morales said, with his usual happy disposition. One corner of his mouth rose as he eyed Paul. "You're dressed pretty fancy for Ballentine. Heading somewhere?"

Paul thought back to his phone conversation with Delia. What had Monsignor Costa overheard? If anything of consequence, he was sure Costa marched over to Morales, immediately filling him in on the news. The two were worse hens than the Ladies' Auxiliary.

"Perhaps you recall, I spoke with my sister yesterday," Paul said, reaching for the kitchen door, a spring in his step.

"Well then, enjoy your day, Father Wainwright." Morales raised his cup. "Cheers."

Grinning, Paul waved as he stepped through the doorway. "Right back at you."

Chapter Four

The Lunch

Delia rolled her eyes as she answered her car's Bluetooth. "Yes, Frank?" she said through gritted teeth.

"What's with the new number? You get a different phone?" Frank didn't wait for a reply. Instead, he demanded, "Where are you?"

"That's none of your business. We aren't together anymore. Remember?" She gripped the steering wheel, knowing if she wasn't careful, Frank would make her pay later. "It's my day off." She let the disdain drip from her voice.

"Well, I have a job to do," Frank spat. She envisioned him pacing his office, his fury growing as he realized he didn't have control over her. "I need you here. Mr. Yamano is asking for you. I need you to do the one thing I *know* you're good at. So get in here. Now."

"I have plans." Delia braced for Frank's next outburst.

"Unacceptable!" Frank barked. "You listen to me. When one of the Dragon's top guests specifically asks the operations manager for a request, I make every effort to accommodate. And, in return, I expect *you* to make every effort to accommodate. So, get your sweet ass over here. Ito Yamano and his guests bring in a lot of money. He's specifically asking for you."

She shuddered, relieved not to have to be stuck with the next several hours of unpleasantness. "I'm busy," Delia snapped. "Abigail and Tawana are working today. Ask them."

"He doesn't want anyone else." Frank's voice grew deeper and his speech slower. "When will you be free? I can tell him maybe later on? This evening perhaps?"

"The next day I work is Wednesday." Delia tightened her fingers around the steering wheel. Her shoulders tensed as she braced herself for Frank's response.

"Wednesday!" Frank roared. "He's asking for you now! He doesn't want Abigail or Tawana. Damnit! This is the second time you've done this to me lately."

If anything positive came from last week's flat tire, it was her broken phone and the subsequent relief from Frank's inability to track her movements. Otherwise, Delia knew he, or someone from the casino, would be hunting her down within minutes, escorting her out of the restaurant, and into Ito Yamano's bed.

"I had a flat tire!" she snapped. "I called you for help. You couldn't be bothered. Why didn't you come take care of it, if me being late for a client was such a big deal?" Delia shifted in her seat, knowing she'd pay a tall price later for her sass. Hoping to mollify him, she said, "Look, on the off chance I have some free time this afternoon, I'll check in. Right now, I'm out of town."

"*Are* you out of town?" Frank hissed. "I expect you to be available when there are certain guests staying here."

"I am well aware of what you expect," she shot back. "However, I was already unavailable when you called. Therefore, I'm not coming in. Had you let me know last night, I understand I would have had to make other arrangements." *But I would have been willing to fake the stomach flu to get out of it if I had to.*

"We'll discuss your conduct later."

"I'm sure we will." She made a face.

Maneuvering her car into the empty parking spot next to Paul's truck, she felt her lips turn into a small smile. Delia slipped the Honda into park. Glancing over, Paul sat in the driver's seat looking into the rearview mirror holding his comb. The waves of his light brown hair sprang back up as fast as he smoothed them down. His hand swept by his face too quickly, knocking his glasses askew.

She suppressed a giggle at Paul's sweet attempt to primp. He was cute and reminded her of someone Hollywood might cast as the attractive college professor. Lunch, and whatever she could do for him afterward, would be worth Frank being angry. And given what a dud Ito Yamano was in the sack, there's no way Paul wouldn't be amazing compared to the casino's high roller.

Leaning forward, she checked her lipstick. "Got to run, Frank. Bye."

***

"So, tell me," Delia said, after they gave the waiter their order. "Why were you on that lonely stretch of Louisiana road last week when you live in Texas?"

Paul smiled, making Delia feel as if she'd known him for several lifetimes. Conversation had been easy between them. She was surprised this far into lunch that he'd made no physical advances, nor had he made any innuendo. In fact, he'd been a complete gentleman, even going so far as to pull out her chair when they sat down. Though the guests at the casino made similar overtures, their motives were orchestrated to show their good breeding. It was an easy contrast. Paul had good breeding and didn't need to prove it.

"I was coming back from Little Rock." He sipped his water before he continued. "I work with . . . well, I work with prisoners in the Ballentine Prison system. There was an incident. A prisoner died. The family asked me to speak at their son's funeral because I had been with him in his final hour."

Delia covered her mouth. "That's terrible. How awful for his family and for you."

She saw a flash in his eyes as he shrugged. "Part of the job."

Leaning forward, her hand hovered above the table, poised to touch Paul's arm. A look of confusion crept across his face. His forehead wrinkled. He leaned back, moving out of her reach while adjusting his glasses. Wanting to save the moment, Delia dabbed her lips with her napkin, meeting his eyes, she offered him a demure smile.

Paul relaxed as the color came back to his face.

Delia asked, "What exactly do you do?"

"Well," Paul started. "I . . . uh, counsel . . . I mean, I work in counseling. Part of what I do is at the prison."

"That's amazing, Paul. Most folks wouldn't be so compassionate or think to be kind to people who are locked up. And you do this willingly?" Delia's eyes widened as she sat back, watching his ears turn pink.

"I think of it more as . . . well, a calling, if you will."

"My point exactly. Your calling is kindness. Isn't that how we met?"

"So it seems." Paul gulped. "Now your turn. What were you doing on that road?"

"Oh," she waved a dismissive hand, "I was visiting my mother. My family's from Lewisville. It's in Arkansas. About an hour from here. One of those wide spots in the road with a single gas station and a Baptist church. It's only crowded during hunting season. That's my drive back to Shreveport. I try to see Mama every month or so. All of us kids moved away. She's alone and starting to slow down. Like all parents, I guess."

As the waiter set down their lunches, Delia reached for her fork. "Looks delicious," she said, eyeing her chopped salad.

Paul cleared his throat. "If you don't mind, I'd like to say a blessing," he said. "I mean, I do this always before I eat."

She gestured as her cheeks grew hot. "Please. By all means."

He made the sign of the cross. Muscle memory from her childhood took over, as she automatically followed along. Delia watched Paul as he offered prayers of thanks for the food, for their new friendship, as well as for those who need compassion. She was still staring after his "amen."

"Are you Catholic?" Paul asked.

She let out a long breath. "I guess. I haven't been to church in years. My granny took me until she died. I was about ten or eleven. I don't remember the prayers or anything. Not sure if God would take me back."

"I . . . I don't think it works that way," Paul replied. He shifted in his chair and chewed a bite of his salad. "What about you? What do you do?"

"Well," Delia began. "I work at the Dragon Casino. It's on the Red River—in the tourist district. One of the newer ones."

"I know where it is. I passed it on the way here. Red glass, tall, flashy."

"That's the one. I'm in customer relations." Delia tilted her chin. "I work with the more elite guests, like a private concierge for the casino's privileged. It's a small department, compared to the other hotel operations."

"Keeping them happy, I suppose." Paul asked, "What kinds of things do you handle?"

If you only knew. "Whatever they need. You know, the usual." She twirled her fork in the air and threw out a jaunty laugh. "Opera tickets. Not that there's much of an opera scene in Shreveport. We aren't exactly in the cultural heart of the South. Generally, the high rollers are men, and they want to make sure their families are entertained. So, I coordinate day care or field trips for their children. I hunted down a Miss Mazey doll once—with the green dress, not the yellow dress—for a client's daughter. I finally found one in South Korea and had it overnighted to our hotel. Found a toy poodle for a wife. Booked tickets to Paris a couple of weeks ago for one guest and his friend." *And Abigail damn well better have had a good time.*

"Wow. Do you meet a lot of elite in the bayou?"

"Usually from Asia and South America. Plus, there are a lot of folks from the area who work in the oil industry. But truthfully, Middle America doesn't exactly flock to Louisiana to gamble."

"Sounds more glamorous than counseling prisoners."

"I bet it feels similar at times. The husband who gambled too much and is looking for a sympathetic ear because his wife is going to kill him when she finds out he's blown their entire savings." Delia pointed her thumb toward her chest. "That's also me."

"What do you say to them?" Paul leaned forward. "I'm curious."

"Really? What can I say?" She shrugged. "Usually, I start with 'be honest' or something like that." *But that's not the kind of sympathy they want.* "You're a counselor. What would you tell them?"

Paul finished chewing. "Probably something along those lines. I'd add that I care about their problem. And then I'd direct them to a Gambler's Anonymous group or someone who is trained to work with addiction.

Maybe suggest that it might soften the blow when they do tell their significant other if they've already sought help."

"Good point. I will add that part. Thank you, Mr. Wainwright. Ah, you are definitely a clever one."

Her phone buzzed. "Please come in. Mr. Yamano is insisting." Delia frowned as she read the text. If Frank was using, "please," the casino's general manager was breathing down his back.

"Do you need to take that?" Paul asked, motioning to Delia's cell.

"No. It's work." She shook her head. "It's my day off. I rarely get one and I want to make the most of it. If I jump every time they want me to come in, I'll never have time to myself." Reaching over, she placed her hand on Paul's arm. His brows curved, while he fumbled with his fork, catching it between his fingers before it hit the floor. She caught his eye. "Besides, I'm having a really nice time."

Paul leaned back while taking a deep breath. The hint of a smile formed on his lips. "I am too." He pushed his glasses further onto his nose while looking at his phone. "I don't have to head back to Ballentine any time soon. If you aren't busy this afternoon, would you like to do something else? I don't know Shreveport, but surely there's something around here. I saw a bowling alley?"

"Bowling?" She let the word roll off her tongue. "That's an idea. It's been a while since I've . . . bowled."

"Well, maybe you aren't dressed for bowling," he conceded.

Delia bit her lip, unsure how to proceed. This wasn't the direction she'd expected lunch to take. Her phone vibrated again. Without checking the text, she tucked it into her purse. "My entire day-off plans consisted of lunch with you, laundry, and grocery shopping. Bowling never would have been on my radar for the afternoon. But what the heck!" Placing her napkin next to her plate she added, "Who'd think to find me there? It'll be fun."

Chapter Five

The Wedding

Paul drove back to Saint Daniel's on Interstate 20, thinking about his afternoon with Delia. Never in his wildest dreams did he imagine he'd have an opportunity to make a friend—because that's all she could ever be—as delightful as her. Catholic priests don't date. They don't marry. And, thanks to a *certain woman*, he'd made a vow of celibacy long before he decided to enter the seminary.

His day with Delia and his Shreveport business finished, Paul experienced an emotional letdown. The temporary reprieve from his memories of the prison riot now over, he watched the endless Interstate, as the guilt and horror of that night almost two weeks earlier returned to haunt him. Days from now he was expected at a hearing, where he would need to recount what he witnessed. Warden Shackleford said they wanted to discuss "lessons learned," so future mistakes could be avoided. As far as Paul was concerned, his biggest mistake was agreeing to negotiate a prison riot in the first place.

Shoving the prison business aside, Paul glanced at the clock on his truck's dashboard. He groaned. *A little after six and another forty miles to go.* The thought of heading back to Saint Daniel's left an unappealing hole in an otherwise enjoyable day. In the last few hours, he'd become addicted to the renewed life Delia breathed into him.

But his chat with Morales that morning came back. Was Father Morales being friendly or was he directed by Monsignor Costa to check on him? Though they'd lived together for years, he couldn't decide if it was common among the three men to discuss what their plans were on their days off, because they rarely went anywhere farther than Tyler.

He strummed his fingers across his steering wheel. "I need another distraction," Paul said aloud, while steering to the road's shoulder. Pulling out his phone, he called Chuck.

***

"Evening, Friar," Chuck said, opening the front door. He handed Paul a longneck while grabbing the pizza box out of his brother's hands. He wore his Tyler EMT work shirt but had changed from boots to flip-flops. "Game's about to start."

Paul took a swig, enjoying the taste of the cold beer, a luxury only to be enjoyed away from Saint Daniel's. One of Costa's rules was no alcohol in the rectory. The monsignor's loophole was to keep a great stash of the good stuff locked away in his office, available for himself and any donor who wanted to write a generous check.

"Who are the Mavericks playing?"

"Suns." Chuck flopped on the couch and motioned for Paul to do the same. "Britt will be here in a bit." He waved his hand around. "She's redecorating."

Paul scanned the room. The walls seemed shinier, but he would have been hard-pressed to say if they were a new color. On the couch lay several small pillows he'd never noticed before, which didn't seem to serve much of a purpose other than making it difficult to sit. Picking up one, he examined it, placing it on the nearby recliner.

Chuck laughed. "Good idea." He tossed the companion pillow across the room. "What's the point? If I'm sleeping on the couch, I need better neck support."

The Mavericks were up by four in the second quarter when Chuck spoke again. Giving Paul a side-long look, he said, "Ally told me what happened."

"Three forms of communication," Paul grumbled, not taking his eyes off the television. "Telephone, telegraph, and tell Ally."

"She means well," Chuck said. "Worries." Before Paul could respond, they heard the outside door creak. "In here, Britt," Chuck called.

"Hey Paul," Brittany said, walking into the room, giving Chuck a kiss, and then offering Paul a hug. She shook her head and pointed at them. "You two could be the twins in the family. Except I'm absolutely certain I've let the better-looking brother get away."

She took a seat on the armrest next to Chuck, leaning into him and rubbing his neck. He slipped his arm around her waist. Paul watched the automatic exchange between the two while imagining wrapping his arm around Delia. The thought surprised him. Paul shook out the notion while letting the guilt for such an idea settle in.

"You can go to hell for flirting with a priest, Babe," Chuck said.

"I'll take my chances."

Paul said, "Good to see you, Britt. Which department are you working in now?"

"Still in the ICU. Nursing shortage there." She eyed him. "You're wearing normal clothes. What have you been doing today?"

"Went to Shreveport," Paul replied. "I ministered in a nursing home this morning. Wasn't ready to go back to the rectory. My day off."

"No nursing homes in Ballentine or Tyler?" Brittany asked. She caught Chuck's eye. "Have you told him?"

He shook his head. "Nope, just drinking beer and watching the game."

"Priests drink beer?" Brittany asked.

"Only if they like beer," Paul said, downing the last quarter of his bottle. He stood, enjoying how the buzz from the alcohol helped him forget the last two weeks. "Anyone want another?"

"Please." Chuck raised his hand.

"None for me, thanks," Brittany said.

Paul couldn't help comparing her to Delia. Brittany was girl-next-door pretty, with straight black hair, blue eyes, and olive skin. Delia was a Southern belle while Brittany was Texan to the core.

"So," Paul started, handing the new bottle to Chuck. "What's new?"

Brittany, with a broad smile on her face, whipped out her left hand and wiggled her fingers. "We're engaged!"

"Congratulations. It's about time you made an honest man out of him," Paul said, shaking his brother's hand. He leaned over and kissed Brittany's cheek. "Welcome to our crazy."

"And . . ." Brittany added, beaming at Chuck, "We're pregnant! Due in November."

Paul coughed out the beer he'd been in the process of swallowing. Chuck threw him a knowing glance. His brother knew those words dusted off memories Paul'd have preferred to stay hidden.

"Wow! What great news!" Paul's voice rose, but he meant every word. Shoving his selfish regret for never being a father deep into his consciousness, he laughed. "Maybe I should marry you right now so you will stop sinning. No reason to wait."

"You could?" Brittany asked. "I hadn't thought about that." She gazed at Chuck. "We weren't really thinking about having a Catholic wedding. No offense. I was raised Southern Baptist."

"Obviously, Chuck isn't a practicing Catholic," Paul pointed out.

"Nope," Chuck said. "But you know, the friar's got a good idea. He's right here. We could get married tonight. Why wait?"

"Well, hold on." Paul extended his palm. He turned to Brittany. "Wouldn't you want your family and a real wedding?"

She shrugged. "My parents are pretty religious. They're gonna flip anyway when they find out I'm knocked up. Plus, they're in Amarillo. They don't know I'm living with Chuck."

"Exactly how is that possible?" Paul sputtered. "You guys have been together for years." He waved his arm around the living room. "You two bought this house, what? Three years ago?" He picked up the throw pillow from the recliner. "Bought these meaningless things. That's a huge commitment. I'm pretty sure your folks probably figured it out."

"You said you could marry us right now? Paulie, are you going to do it or what?" Chuck asked.

"Yeah, Paul. Better do it before I decide I want to go after the better-looking brother," Brittany added.

"You don't have a marriage license. The State of Texas says you have to wait seventy-two hours after obtaining your license to get married. So, I guess the earliest I could marry you is three days after that."

Paul knew Monsignor Costa's strict rules for his priests and for the couples who sought out weddings at Saint Daniel's. A minimum of six months of premarital classes would be required, even if it wasn't a

Catholic wedding. In addition to strengthening the couple's relationship, he was aware these practices were used to augment future membership and potential counseling if need be—two additional revenue sources. That information was given to the diocese and used as partial justification for having three priests at a tiny country church that only needed one.

Brittany slid between the brothers and rested her elbow on Paul's shoulder. "What about this." She drummed her fingers on his upper arm. "You marry us right now. We get the license tomorrow and then we put the correct date on it?"

Paul watched the Mavericks' forward dunk the ball, get fouled, and make the extra point. The disappointment he'd felt earlier while driving back from spending the day with Delia returned, bringing with it the now-familiar emptiness. This hadn't been the kind of distraction he had in mind when he'd called his brother. But then again, Paul's job—his calling—was to save souls. There was a baby involved—one who was wanted. One who would be loved and would have a committed mother and father. Chuck and Brittany were compatible. What would this slight deviation matter?

Their eternal salvation. A wanted child. That's what mattered.

"Yes, technically I can marry you." He drew in a breath. "It's against the rules in my diocese, not to mention there's probably some law about purposely putting the wrong date on an official State of Texas document. You know, fraud." Paul craned his head toward the ceiling. "But fine. Bring me the license. I'll be in Thursday morning." Pointing at them, he added, "I'm putting Thursday's date on it, and you are on your own for finding witnesses."

Brittany threw her arms around Paul. He managed a halfhearted smile, patting her hand while imagining his brother as a father. She squealed, "Thank you! I'll come see you. Thursday's perfect. I'm off that day."

Chuck whipped out his phone. "Go change your clothes, Britt. I'm calling Allison. We'll never hear the end of this if we don't invite her."

"She can't come here," Paul said. "The kids are probably in bed."

"You're right." Chuck conceded. "I'll text her and let her know we're on our way."

Chapter Six

The Executive Concierge Desk

Late Thursday morning, Paul sat in his office, working on his sermon for Saturday night's Mass. He tapped his fingers on the desk as he closed his eyes, fighting writer's block. Generally, Matthew's Gospel, *Treasures in Heaven,* resonated a great deal of strength for him. Today he contemplated if the treasures he thought he stored up for Heaven were the wrong ones.

Already, the week caused a great deal of adrenaline whiplash. Given the first two days of the week were Paul's normal days off, on Tuesday he found other ways to busy himself and stayed clear of his office. Costa and Morales continued to circle like sharks, treating him as if he were chumming the water while he sat in the living room of the rectory pretending to read while thinking back to his afternoon with Delia at the bowling alley and the friendly banter they'd shared. Several times, he considered calling her, just to say hello. However, he knew with his two fellow priests hovering, they'd hear everything and get the wrong idea.

Wednesday morning, Paul found a small stack of retreat pamphlets on his desk. He asked Annie about them. The church secretary said they came from Monsignor Costa, who thought he might be interested. After giving them a cursory scan and reaffirming he didn't need a retreat with more time alone with his memories, he shoved them into the back of his filing cabinet.

After the hearing at the Ballentine Correctional Facility Wednesday afternoon, Paul had plenty of time to think. What Warden Shackleford sold as a friendly conversation with routine questions blossomed into an inquisition. Foster admitted to killing Armetta in a heated argument, although his lawyer insisted the act was committed in self-defense. His guilt or innocence would be resolved in a court trial later in the year.

The prison committee wanted to know more about the origins of the fight. Foster said it began because of his outrage at Armetta's violent treatment of the guards. One was still in a coma in a Houston hospital. Another guard lost an eye, half of his spleen, and a lung. The third was not expected to walk again. Foster stated he feared Paul or himself would be next in line for Armetta's wrath.

Even with Marvin Foster's admission, the prison council asked more questions of Paul than he expected. Did he have any animosity toward Armetta? Did he see weapons on either man? Did he aid and abet either side in the fight?

His answers never crossed into the blurred lines of Foster's confession. However, when the chairwoman asked if he knew prior if Foster planned to murder Armetta, Paul replied it had never crossed his mind, again second-guessing how he missed such obvious cues.

Some committee members mused whether Paul should continue his ministry, under the circumstances. Both Martinez and Shackleford came to his defense, while demanding the comment be stricken from the record. Even Foster jumped in from the back of the room protesting the suggestion, with his lawyer working to calm him down.

Now, with his sermon staring at him, Paul let his hand hover above his phone once again, daring himself to contact Delia. He'd already texted her yesterday, right after the hearing, asking how her week was going. Pleased she'd replied so quickly, Paul checked his calendar for the following week to see if he had time to make the drive back to Shreveport. However, he hadn't invited her to lunch again. Just yet. "Thou shall work first. Play later," he muttered.

Returning to his notes, he planted his hands on each side of his head, praying for insight. Still unsuccessful, Paul stretched, playing his usual game of lengthening his arms until the tips of his middle fingers could touch both sides of his office at once. Finally, deciding the avocado-green walls held no more insight into Scripture, he sent Delia a text, snatched his notes, opting to move his thoughts and unfinished homily into the Saint Daniel's chapel for a moment of prayer and quiet contemplation.

Costa waved as Paul walked by his doorway. "Father Wainwright, do you have a second?"

"Of course." Paul rustled his papers so the monsignor wouldn't think he had time for a friendly chit-chat. Stepping into Costa's office, an audible sigh escaped before Paul could hold it back. He gazed out the senior priest's window, which brought in ample sunlight and overlooked the Saint Daniel's grounds. Jealousy flashed through him. "Looks like a beautiful day."

"Agreed." Costa nodded. "Father, I was wondering," he began, putting his fingers together. "How have you been?"

"Fine, sir." He shrugged. "Something on your mind?"

"We were concerned Monday night."

Paul offered a small smile. "Yes, it's unfortunate you and Father Morales didn't get my text stating I was staying in Tyler until Tuesday morning."

Costa nodded. "Indeed." He continued, "I don't think I've seen that woman you were with before."

Paul froze. "Woman?" The question left his mouth as a thin breath.

"Today. At the Wagon Wheel."

"That's my sister-in-law, Brittany." He gave a light laugh as he relaxed his muscles. "She stopped by this morning for a visit. It's a shame you didn't come by and join us. I would love to have introduced you."

"I didn't realize Chuck had gotten married."

Paul shrugged. "They eloped recently."

Monsignor shook his head. "I'm positive you did your best to convince them they should have been married in the Church. Though we both know Chuck is aware of this. Better for everyone." He grabbed his pencil and jotted a note on his blotter. "When you have a moment, would you please get me your brother's address? I'd like to send them a congratulations card."

"Will do. I'm certain he'd love to hear from you."

Costa sat back in his chair. "Did you have a chance to review those retreats Annie left for you?"

Paul forced a smile. "At this time, I don't think—"

"I understand. Like I said the other day, if you need time off, please take it."

"Thank you. Working is therapy." Paul locked his gaze outside, staring at downtown Ballentine. He turned back to Monsignor. "I do have a request and I'm happy to pay for the cost of the materials, Sir."

Costa raised an eyebrow.

"I'd like to add a window to my office. It would be nice to look outside occasionally when I'm working and check out God's creation."

"I'll run it by the bishop. See what he says. It wouldn't be much of a view. What's back there? The parking lot?" Monsignor frowned, shaking his head. He pushed his glasses to the top of his nose while neatening a stack of papers on his desk. "Let me ask you this, how did your hearing go yesterday?"

Paul shrugged. "As expected, I suppose. I didn't enjoy reliving the experience."

"So, now is probably not the best time to tell you this, as I'm sure you'd like to move on." He blew out a breath, letting his shoulders go lax. "The bishop wants you to meet with him on Friday before your basketball practice. I believe he'd like to discuss what happened the night of the riot."

Paul tightened his jaw. "I don't suppose you could convince him otherwise? The guards were tortured. Another man lost his life. I really don't want to talk about it."

"I did suggest you might feel that way. He didn't change his mind."

***

Delia sat at the Executive Concierge Desk on the twelfth floor of the Dragon Casino and Resort rubbing her temples, hoping she'd have a moment alone to refocus before her next work assignment. She'd spent most of her Thursday morning shift setting up a New Orleans weekend trip for the wives of two high rollers. With the usual transport service the Dragon hired for such excursions unavailable, she'd put extra effort into locating a charter flight, making sure these two guests were gone no later than after breakfast tomorrow because Gordon Cranston's mistress arrived Friday at noon.

The Adairs posed a bigger challenge. Mrs. Adair stopped by the desk every hour, micromanaging Delia. What was the sheet thread count at the New Orleans Hotel? What kind of car would be picking her and Mrs. Cranston up from the airport? Had reservations been made for a pre-dinner massage on Saturday? If not, why?

Mrs. Adair's need for control and her husband's future motives did nothing to make Delia's job smoother. If the wife wasn't at the Executive Concierge Desk demanding lemongrass smoothies be added to her New Orleans room service menu, Mr. Adair behaved as if his wife had already left town. Howie, as he'd instructed Delia and Abigail to call him, orbited by twice that afternoon to say hello, making no secret of his expectations.

Additionally, Frank spent the morning peacocking around the twelfth floor, while barking at the girls at the desk. Delia heard he'd done the same Monday afternoon while she'd been out with Paul. Twice during the last hour, Frank walked by, shot an insult at Delia, and stormed off to his office as one of the high rollers strolled into the lounge. His last pointed comment before Mrs. Adair interrupted with a demand for her afternoon tea at the New Orleans Ritz tomorrow to include gluten-free beignets, included grabbing Delia's arm, twisting it backward, and informing her they'd be discussing her conduct from Monday's phone call.

Mr. Adair happened to be her next probable work assignment. Abigail's monthly blood test results hadn't arrived, leaving Delia as the likely candidate for Howie. The consensus from the women at the Executive Concierge Desk was he'd be a fine specimen for such endeavors. And, as far as Delia was concerned, better than Frank, who still showed up at her front door at all hours of the day, expecting sex on demand. Later that afternoon, when he could sneak away from Mrs. Adair, Delia needed to schedule a short conference—standard protocol—with Howie about the Dragon's

"Premium Platinum Package" he'd selected, which included several hours of her weekend.

None of this interested her right now. Since Monday's lunch and bowling, Delia continued thinking about Paul Wainwright. She'd heard from him once, a quick text Wednesday afternoon saying hello and asking about her week. Frustrated, her mind drifted from Howie and her job responsibilities then back to wondering if Paul would ask her out again.

Abigail nudged her and pointed toward the security monitor. "Looks like Howie is heading this way."

Delia held back a groan while grabbing her purse. "Abs, I'm going on break and try to beat the lunch rush. I need to grab a bite to eat. Can you see if Mr. Adair needs an *immediate* something? Otherwise, I'll be back in a few minutes. If your blood test results come back, book him for yourself for the weekend. I don't mind."

"Sure thing," Abigail said. "Pick me up a mineral water?"

She blew a kiss over her shoulder while hurrying to the elevator. "You got it."

Relieved to be away from the mad scramble of scheduling New Orleans tour guides and last-minute private air travel, Delia sat with her soup and a magazine in the Dragon's food court. As a bonus, Frank's aversion to counter-service restaurants made it a quiet place for her to clear her mind.

However, she knew her freedom from him would be short-lived. Memories of Frank throughout the past several years showing up at coffee shops, yoga classes, and even doctor appointments, dragging her to the twelfth floor of the Dragon Casino for "client meetings" caused her to tremble. How could she have wasted so many years with him? How could she have ever thought she loved this man?

Delia eyed her new cell phone. So far, she'd kept it with her, prolonging the inevitable reality. Eventually he'd snatch it. In the past, she thought of him tracking her as a mere annoyance, just part of being Frank's on-again, off-again, and member of the Executive Concierge Desk—though he didn't do this to any of the other girls on the twelfth floor. However, this past week, Delia reconsidered.

After one date with Paul, she'd discovered another kind of man, one not like Frank or the Dragon's high rollers. Even if Paul didn't turn out to be *the one*, there could be others like him. That kind of man should be given a second look.

As Delia gazed into the distance, listening to the bells on the casino floor, in the corner of her eye, she saw Howie Adair walking through the casino, beelining toward the food court. *Crap.* Her phone buzzed. Abigail's text read, "Howie wants YOU, Babe."

Another text came in. "Sorry I couldn't ask sooner. Are you free Monday? I'm coming back to Shreveport."

She gave a girlish squeal. Joy spread through Delia, even if prudence suggested it might be premature to get her hopes up about Paul. Looking up, she saw Howie crossing the casino floor, zeroing in on her. She sent a quick reply. "I'm all yours Monday." She opted not to send a topless picture. Too soon? Not necessarily. She'd sent those many times, long before a first date. But Paul . . . he was special.

Howie reached the food court and waved in her direction. She flashed him a smile, waved back, and then eyed her soup. Her stomach growled, bringing her back to reality. Before giving him anything, she needed lunch.

But first, Delia wanted to continue her new habit. Making the sign of the cross, she bowed her head and began to pray. When she finished, she scanned the area, relieved to see Howie had disappeared.

***

Saturday afternoon, Delia arrived for her shift at the Dragon with Abigail greeting her at the Executive Concierge Desk. "Here are the current demands for today," she said, handing her the list of guest requests from the Dragon's elite clientele.

"Really, we need to find Peruvian guava jam? Where do we get that in Shreveport?"

"Or," Abigail countered, holding up a finger, "what we need to do is find marmalade, blend it a bit more until it's smooth, and have a graphic designer make a label. I called Whole Foods. They're sending us four jars of marmalade and four jars of peach preserves. We'll mix them."

"Thank you, Abs, you're a lifesaver." Covering her mouth, Delia smothered a yawn.

"Howie keep you out past your bedtime?"

She wrinkled her nose. "Not too late. But the asshole gave me a hickey. What is this? Seventh grade? I have a date Monday. I don't want my *real date* to see this."

Abigail glanced at her friend. "I don't see a mark."

"It's under my clothes."

"Ah . . . Well, I guess I know what you won't be doing Monday, unless you want to come clean to your date."

Delia shook her head. "Oh well. It's a second date anyway. I guess we'll be one of those clichéd couples and wait till the third one before we get down to business."

"You're quite the lady, Delia Hargrove." Abigail laughed, picking up the ringing desk phone. "Dragon Casino Executive Concierge." She listened and then purred, "Please hold." Turning to Delia she said, "It appears your performance last night made a lasting impression on Howie. He's requesting your presence in his room as soon as possible."

Delia sighed, reached into the bottom drawer of the desk, and pulled out a handful of condoms, shoving them into her purse. She slipped on a gold-plated bracelet and necklace, then inserted matching earrings. Executive Concierge Desk employees wore specialized jewelry with built-in alarms that signaled security in the event Howie or any high roller got out of hand.

"Please tell him I'll be right there."

Howie Adair answered before Delia finished knocking. "Come in, Denise." Honey dripped from his voice.

Delia thought about correcting him but decided against it. "Hello, Mr. Adair. How can I help you?" she asked with a plastered smile.

The man ogled her while she suppressed the urge to roll her eyes. Instead, she acted as if she had no idea what on Earth he wanted.

"Call me Howie, Darlin'."

She batted her eyelashes. "Well then, *Howie*, how can I help you?"

He held up two tickets to the 1980s guitarist who'd been headlining for the past two months. "Would you like to accompany me tonight?" Howie waggled his eyebrows.

Not really, I've seen the show six times. "Oh, I'd love to." Clapping her hands, she bounced on the balls of her feet as she added in her best Southern drawl, "Really? You'd like to take me? I'm honored."

Howie's eyes devoured her. Delia recognized his hungry expression.

"Of course, Darlin'. A beautiful and sexy lady like you on my arm? Who wouldn't want to be with you?"

He strode to an end table. A large pile of colorful casino chips lay next to an oversized vase of orange and yellow gladiolas. "After you left last night, I did well at the tables. You've gotta be my lucky charm." Selecting two chips, he grabbed Delia's purse from her hands, slipping the money inside. "Figure you're worth ten grand. You earned it."

Delia fluttered her hand to her chest. "Thank you."

Howie handed her back her purse. "Bet you never got a tip like that before."

"Oh never," she lied. Leaning forward, Delia placed her fingertips on his shoulder. She batted her lashes. "That's so generous, Howie."

He gazed at her hand. Licking his lips he declared, "But before our show, I wouldn't mind a repeat of yesterday. Wish my wife had moves like yours."

Laughing, Delia tossed back her hair. "Well, you seem to bring out the woman in me."

"So glad to hear it, Darlin'. Now then, let's get you naked."

Closing her eyes, she felt the slight tug of the dress's zipper and then the feeling of cool air on her shoulders. She conjured an image of Paul's face as her dress hit the floor.

Chapter Seven

The Dance

"So, tell me about your week," Paul began as they strolled along the downtown river walk, enjoying the morning sunshine. Blooming pink and white dogwoods lined the path, dappling the ground with an even mix of shadow and sunlight. Behind them, the city's casinos towered, shielding them from the rest of Shreveport, as if they were in their own world. A gentle breeze picked up a strand of Delia's hair. He watched her flutter her fingers to her cheek, tucking it behind her ear while making a quick patting motion to ensure the rest of her locks were still in place.

"Nothing exciting. I worked Saturday. You know, the usual . . ." She waved her hand in front of her. "On Sunday, I went to Lewisville to visit my mother. Great to spend time with her. I'd been there twice in a month." She added, "No flat tire this time."

"Does your mom have any other family who live nearby?"

"I have a brother and sister. They live closer to Mama than I do. Both are a half hour away in opposite directions. Tommy lives in Texarkana. He has a job at the recycling plant. Maddy's the baby. She's a junior in Magnolia, at Southern Arkansas University. Getting her degree in accounting."

"How about you? Did you go to college?"

Delia shook her head. "Oh no. Maddy's the smart one. I'm so proud of her for working hard in high school and getting a scholarship."

Paul stopped. He raised one eyebrow. "I believe your sister isn't the only one with the brains in your family."

She glanced at Paul. In a hoarse whisper, she asked, "Are you saying you think I'm smart?"

"Well, . . . in the time I've spent with you, I'd have to say absolutely."

Delia studied her sandals. "Nobody's ever told me I'm smart before," she murmured. "Everyone says I have a pretty face. That's why I work at the Dragon." She waved her hand. "Never mind that . . . But even my teachers . . . nobody expected much from me."

Paul said, "Well, I must say, you also do have a pretty face." He watched as Delia's nose and cheeks reddened. "But you are obviously living proof one can be lovely and intelligent at the same time."

Covering her mouth, Delia stifled a giggle. "I . . . well . . ." She pivoted on the balls of her feet toward the river and then circled back to Paul. "Thank you. I don't know . . . Part of me is flattered you think I'm lovely. It means something special coming from you. But even more, I'm touched you think I'm smart."

"Oh, I know you're bright. I can prove it." Paul rocked back on his heels, giving her a wink. "You agreed to spend the day with me. All kidding aside, yes, you are indeed, without a doubt, intelligent."

Delia, with her shoulders back and her face toward the sky, laughed her melodious laugh. "You've made my week."

"You should give yourself a bit more credit," Paul stated. "By the way, how's your mother?"

"She's doing pretty good, but mostly lonely. I took her to town to go to church and to take care of her grocery shopping. Then I helped her clean her yard," Delia said. "We planted flowers. Probably a little late in the season for verbena, but she likes them."

"Sounds like my weekend. Grocery shopping and church. No yard work, but I had basketball practice."

He watched Delia out of the corner of his eye as she moved along the walkway. Her sashaying hips made her green sundress swish. He couldn't decide which urge felt stronger: to slide his arm around her waist or to place his hand on the small of her back. He stopped mid-step, struck by the brash thoughts that seemed to have tiptoed into his head from nowhere.

Delia looked up but he didn't catch her eye. "I'm sure there was more excitement than grocery shopping," Delia challenged, nudging him with her shoulder.

The spot on his arm tingled from her momentary touch. Paul found that he wished she'd make the same movement again. He stepped backward and shoved his fists into his pockets. "Actually, when I left you last Monday, I did have a bit of excitement. After I left Shreveport, I drove to my brother's house in Tyler. We watched the Mavericks game. I found out my brother's girlfriend is pregnant. She's due in November."

"Oh, how wonderful! Congratulations to them." Delia clasped her hands. "Call me old-fashioned, but are they getting married? I mean, there's a baby on the way."

Paul jutted his chin in her direction. "Agreed. This is where it got exciting. We went to my sister's house that night, around nine—she also lives in Tyler—Allison got to be the maid of honor and her sons were Chuck's groomsmen."

"And you? What did you do?"

"Oh," Paul said, realizing he'd backed himself into a corner. "I . . . well . . . I, uh, ended up marrying them."

"You married them?" Delia asked, not masking the awe in her voice. "You can do that? Did you take a class or something?"

"Yes . . .You . . . you could say so," he stammered. "I'm able to, well . . . marry people."

"You're full of surprises." She leaned over, squeezing his arm.

Paul closed his eyes, relishing the intimacy of Delia's touch and recognizing he shouldn't. *Tell her your calling!* He shut out the cautioning voices bellowing in his head. As he opened his lids, he smothered the much louder thoughts, which were giving him several more creative and appealing ideas, deciding instead he had the discipline and patience to exercise his vow of celibacy.

Saying a quick prayer for guidance, Paul glanced up, thankful for an instant reprieve. A crowd had formed around a four-piece brass band performing next to the walkway. He gestured in their direction. "They're good."

"Casino musicians." She pointed to their handmade sign. "Mondays are slow. They come out here to perform for the crowds and make a few bucks."

"You know, we should help them out."

Tossing a five in the donation box, Paul tapped the handwritten sign, which read, "*Five dollars, for a dance.*" The trumpet player gave him a nod and said something to the rest of the musicians. The music turned from Dixieland jazz to swing.

Paul's mouth spread into a shy smile as he extended his arm. "Warning, I'm a little rusty."

Delia lowered her eyes. "I'll take my chances, Mr. Wainwright."

Seizing his opportunity, he slipped his hand behind Delia's waist, letting his fingertips gently press into the small of her back. As the music came to life, he savored his slight victory of having an opportunity to innocently touch her.

The band played "In the Mood," while Paul twirled her, indulging in Delia's girlish laughter and her womanly form. Enjoying the smell of her vanilla perfume, he worked to commit the moment to memory. The music rang in his ears, drowning out the cheers from the sizable audience growing around them.

"You are better than you think," Delia laughed, squeezing his hand. As the song and the clapping died down, she grabbed his fingers with the confidence of a Southern belle who'd worked the pageant circuit. "Take a bow," she ordered, smiling at the crowd.

Paul permitted his hand to linger a beat longer in hers while his heart thumped through his chest and into his ears. *Tell her! Tell her now!* He brushed away his internal monologue, giving a quick prayer for strength and guidance. Untangling himself while turning to Delia, he said, "I'm hungry."

***

They sat in the back of a 24-hour coffee shop. The suggestion came from Delia, which surprised Paul, given the place reminded him of a dumpier version of the Wagon Wheel. "You mentioned your mother. What about your father?" Paul asked, taking a bite of his sandwich.

Delia shrugged. "I don't know him. Tommy, Maddy, and I all have different fathers. None of them stuck around very long."

"That's too bad. I'm sorry to hear that."

"My father's name is Evan. Mama didn't know his last name. Miller or Minor—something with an M. He worked as a logger in the southern

Arkansas camps one year and ran off when he found out Mama was carrying me."

She continued, "I remember Tommy's dad." Delia shuddered. "A mean drunk. Mama couldn't get rid of him fast enough. And with Maddy, Mama fooled around with a married man. Plus, he's a Baptist preacher." She chuckled. "Can you imagine? A man of the cloth."

Paul gulped. "How unfortunate."

"What about you? Did you grow up in Texas?"

"I did. Tyler, Texas. None of us ventured far from home."

"I take it you have a brother and sister, too?" Delia asked.

"Yes," Paul said. "We're ten months apart."

"Wow. Three babies in twenty months. Your mother must've had her hands full."

"She did. But she had all of us in ten months. Allison is four minutes older than me." Paul lowered his eyelids, straightening his brow. "And I promise you, she acts like she's the oldest."

Delia clasped her hands. "You're a twin! Too bad Allison wasn't a boy. Then you could have switched places in class."

Paul chuckled, trying to imagine Ally breaking any rules as a kid. "Allison never would have done something along those lines. Even now, she's big on not getting into trouble. Chuck, however, he's ten months younger. He usually had no problem bending a rule or two."

"An Irish twin."

"Chuck and I passed for the Wainwright twins when we were kids. But I'm three inches taller." He gave her a lopsided grin. "And frankly, better looking."

"And your parents? What about them?"

He turned away, deciding how much personal history he wanted to share. Finally, he settled on: "They died when Ally and I were twenty. It'll be fifteen years on May 17, later this month."

"Oh Paul," Delia gasped. "How awful." She reached for his arm.

As the warmth of her touch spread through Paul, he realized that since the horrible day he'd walked into his parents' home and discovered their mangled bodies, nobody other than Allison and Chuck ever offered him any physical comfort over his loss. Closing his eyes, he soaked in the healing Delia radiated.

Paul placed his hand on top of hers. Delia opened her fingers, letting his slide in between. "Thank you," he said, relieved she didn't ask for details.

She gave him a sympathetic smile. "Do you do anything for them? Like in remembrance?"

"On All Souls Day, of course."

She tilted her head. "When?"

"November 2nd."

"Oh, right. It's a Catholic holiday. But I mean, do you go to the graveyard and put down flowers?"

Paul, obliging his cautionary voices once again, disentangled his hand from hers while leaning back in his seat. She followed, crossing her legs.

"We do. I'll request a Mass be said for them."

"Well, let me ask you. What is one activity you liked to do with your folks? Either of them? Or both?"

Paul considered. "I have fond memories of Dad, Chuck, and me fishing," he said. "We'd take the boat out to Lake Palestine or even Caddo Lake. Spend the day out there catching

bass . . . The last time was spring break. Two months later, my folks passed."

Delia leaned forward and tapped the table. "That settles it. Let's go fishing the next time you're in Shreveport. In their honor." She added, "Let me ask you something else. Did you have anything in mind for this afternoon, or do you need to head back to Ballentine?"

"Honestly, I did not. I don't know Shreveport. I'm open to suggestions."

"I have passes for the movie theater," Delia offered. "Is a movie too weird?"

"A movie sounds great." An uncomfortable expression crossed his face. "But if it's okay with you, I don't go to R-rated movies. No reason to watch gratuitous violence or sex."

"Oh, wow. Never thought about it. But that's not a problem." Delia pulled out her phone. "Let's see . . . You know what? The theater on Ashbrook? They host Classic Movie Monday. What's 'gratuitous' in this case? This week's film is *Arsenic and Old Lace*."

"Never saw it."

She shook her head. "No gratuitous sex. No blood. But a lot of dying and . . . I don't want to give away the plot. Good movie. They change the film every week. The casino always has passes."

***

On the drive back to Ballentine, Paul spent the first forty miles in prayer, thanking the Almighty for his life, which allowed him to serve others in a unique and righteous way while making him feel needed and appreciated. The same life also brought him Delia, the distraction he'd asked God for, two weeks earlier.

Though grateful for his new friend, he recognized at some point, he owed it to Delia to tell her what he did for a living. But right now, it seemed too soon. After all, there was no romantic connection. Sure, he felt an attraction, though it would be presumptuous to assume she felt the same way. However, that didn't stop the twinge of guilt from eking out, reminding him there were lines he should not cross in thought, word, or deed. In the past, he ran into other Catholic priests who crossed lines they shouldn't have. Sometimes when priests were together, the topic of clergy having secret lives arose.

"I can do this," Paul resolved, watching the white lines on the Interstate fly by.

He flexed his fingers while promising himself he would strive to keep his thoughts and motives pure. Because Paul knew what he had wasn't a secret life, but merely an innocent friendship with a delightful woman who made him remember he was still a man.

Chapter Eight

The Humiliation

Friday night, the priests in the Diocese of Tyler lost their annual basketball tournament to this year's seminarians by a score of 105 to 71. Ally, her sons, and Brittany, as well as almost every member of the clergy who could make it, watched the trouncing from the bleachers of Tyler's Saint Monica's Cathedral.

"What happened, Uncle Paul?" Archie asked when the game ended. "Mom said you thought you were going to win."

"I believe the way it is normally described is the padres had their asses handed to them by the padawans," Brittany said, giving Paul a towel.

"That's the way some might say it." Paul mopped the sweat from his forehead. He drank from a water bottle Allison handed him, then splashed a bit more on his face. "I'd like to think we were humbled by the seminarians."

"Go with that. Much better." Allison patted Paul on the back. "Though I'd say humiliated is a better description."

"What's a seminarian anyway?" Archie asked.

"It's a priest in training. They go to a special priest school. Sometimes God sends men there." She eyed her twin. "And sometimes men think He sends them there."

Paul shot Allison a dirty glare.

She turned to Brittany. "Y'all want to meet at our house for pizza?" Ruffling Archie's hair, she added, "Go find your brothers."

Brittany said, "Pizza sounds good. Chuck's off his shift in an hour. I'll text him." She gestured to Paul, adding, "You coming?"

His chest sank as he glanced across the court. Costa and Morales stood in the corner of the gym, talking to the bishop. For the past two weeks, he'd managed to avoid Bishop Vance's summoning. "Hopefully," he replied. "Maybe if we leave now."

Ally glanced in the direction of the three priests. She waved at Monsignor Costa, who waved back with a broad smile. Turning to Paul she said, "You think they are talking about you? Don't you?"

"Can we discuss this later?"

"Maybe they're talking about all the money the tournament made for the Tyler Women's Clinic." Allison laughed. "You gotta admit, Paulie, being the captain of the team has some perks. Nice job with that."

"Thanks," Paul said while poking his head through the neck hole in his sweatshirt.

Allison tilted her head toward the priests. Her tone grew somber. "But you know what I think? They are discussing the riot."

"I don't want to talk about this. Not now," Paul grumbled, sliding his arms into the sleeves.

"Suit yourself. But I'm not going to let this go," Allison singsonged.

Paul replied in the same voice as his sister, "I know you won't, but I wish you would."

"Maybe you could enlighten me?" Brittany suggested.

"Be happy to," Ally said to Brittany. She added, "Paulie, they are heading this way."

He took a step toward the gym's doors. Placing his hand on Allison's back, he said, "Get the boys. I'll meet you there."

"Father Wainwright!" Costa's voice came from across the court.

"See you when you're done, Paulie. Come on, Britt."

***

Monday morning, dressed in his short-sleeve clergy shirt, Paul sat in the lobby outside Bishop Vance's office. He continued to tug on his clerical collar, just to make sure he didn't choke.

When he'd called, saying he'd need to postpone their fishing trip a couple of hours, Delia said she didn't mind. She had nothing going on either Monday or Tuesday. Paul assured her his work meeting in Tyler wouldn't last too long.

Delia's grace toward him sparked an idea. Reaching out to All Saints Catholic Church in Shreveport, Paul asked if there was room to bunk in the rectory, a custom extended to traveling priests. The staff at All Saints welcomed him, offering Paul a comfortable bed and a full refrigerator.

"Sit down, Father," Bishop Vance said, motioning toward the empty chair while settling in across from Paul.

"Thank you," Paul replied, keeping the frustration of Vance's twenty-minute tardiness out of his voice. "You wanted to see me?"

Bishop Vance demonstrated no hurry to push the conversation to the purpose of their meeting. Instead, he began with the usual pleasantries, inquiring about Paul's health, the unseasonably cool spring, and the unfortunate outcome of the priest-seminarian basketball game. When those topics were exhausted, Vance shifted to the Mavericks' chance for the finals and then to a prediction of how the Rangers might do this season.

Paul weathered the questions, waiting for Vance to get to the point. When it appeared the bishop could go no farther with anything mundane, he adjusted his reading glasses onto his nose. Opening a manila folder with, *Wainwright, Paul M.*, the bishop began leafing through his personnel file.

The rickety clock sitting on the bishop's credenza went past twelve twice before Vance spoke again. "You've been with Saint Daniel's seven years. Generally, priests are moved after six, Father. Will you remind me why you weren't transferred?"

"Yes. Monsignor Costa had a heart attack about eighteen months ago. Under the circumstances, you and the monsignor thought it would be prudent for me to stay on. Plus, I started the worship and counseling ministry at the Ballentine Correctional Facility a year earlier. I asked for time to get that going before being moved to a new parish."

"Oh, I remember," Vance said, with a trace of a smile. He leafed through a few more papers before he glanced at Paul. "Now that Monsignor Costa has recovered, how do you feel about possibly taking another assignment?"

"Do you have any place in mind?"

Vance shook his head. "Not really. I have no plans at this time. The reason I'm asking is because, well, Monsignor Costa seems to think you could use some distance from the prison . . . and that unfortunate night."

Paul caught himself raising his eyebrows. He bit down on his molars, hoping to diffuse the intense anger brewing when the subject of the riot came up. "I'd like to stay at Saint Daniel's for now. The prison ministry is important work. I feel . . . called. There are programs to help rehabilitate prisoners, but unless the incarcerated truly understand salvation, anything they do after serving their time doesn't necessarily have as much of a lasting effect. There are studies that show—"

Vance interrupted, waving his hand. "What you are saying is all reasonable and I can see you've given this some thought. Perhaps your replacement could pick up where you left off."

Paul leaned back in his chair. "Replacement? You just said you don't have any plans to transfer me at this time. Is there a problem? Monsignor and Father Morales haven't suggested there's an issue with my performance. I'm well respected by the parishioners—at least to my knowledge. Attendance at my Masses is high. My plate collection numbers are good. Dare I say, even better than Father Morales's and Monsignor Costa's combined. I've offered to sit on the Parish Council." Paul ran his hand through his hair. "Sir, I serve throughout the community, not just in the prison. The project for the unwed mothers, the Saint Vincent dePaul Society that I—"

The bishop waved him off. "No, that's not it at all. Monsignor has never once suggested you have been anything but an exemplary priest. It's . . . well . . . I do wish he'd speak with you about this." Vance sighed. "Costa is under the impression you aren't happy with him. Or more to the point, you aren't *happy*. Like you are in a spiritual drought. It's common. We all go through one on occasion."

Paul didn't mask his surprise. He said, "I assure you, Sir, nothing could be further from the truth. I admire Monsignor Costa. He's been a mentor to me for as long as I can remember, long before I joined the seminary. A friend to my family when I was growing up. I feel blessed to be able to serve with him." Paul shrugged. "I've had a rough few weeks. The riot was a sucker punch. I won't agree to negotiate another situation of that nature."

Vance shut the folder. He opened his desk drawer, dropped the file inside, and closed the drawer with a solid thud, as he threw Paul a sharp look. "There's no reason to be extreme, Father Wainwright," the bishop said. "After all, we are called to serve. You played an extraordinary role, saving the lives of those prison guards. There's no question you should step up again if another situation were to come up. I would expect nothing less."

"Yes, sir," Paul muttered, while curling his fingers around his knees, his knuckles, white.

Vance continued, "I can only imagine what you witnessed. Monsignor told me he's urging you to take some time off."

"'Urging' might be a bit of a stretch."

"Have you thought about maybe a true vacation? I think you might wish to reconsider. And if not now, at a later date, a retreat might do you well."

"Thank you. I'll think about it." Paul glanced at his phone.

"Father, Monsignor Costa wants to respect your privacy about the riot. He and Father Morales both have mentioned the experience seems to have moved you. They have shared their concerns with me," Vance said. "The clergy wish to take care of our own. Tyler may have a population of more than one hundred thousand, but in many respects, it is a small town."

"I appreciate that," Paul said, standing to leave. "If you'll excuse me. I really must—"

Vance cleared his throat while clasping his hands on his desk. His voice softened. "Paul, I remember your folks. Amazing people. Your mother taught at Saint Joseph's. Eleventh grade English, if I recall."

Paul nodded as he slipped behind his chair. "Monsignor Costa was the principal—and basketball coach—while my sister, brother, and I attended."

"Yes. And I remember watching your basketball games. Even back then Monsignor bragged about you—of course, he still does. He said you were one of the finest athletes Saint Joseph's ever had. He said you had a promising athletic career in front of you, if you wanted it," Vance said.

"I don't think I ever took pro basketball as a career seriously. It paid for college." Paul backed up, moving two more strides toward the doorway.

Vance continued, "I remember you and your family when I was pastor at Our Lady of Guadalupe. You and little Charlie were altar servers."

"I'll have to remind my brother someone remembers him as Charlie." Paul smiled as he extended his left arm, gripping the doorjamb. "He goes by Chuck now. But he's still shorter than me."

Bishop Vance shook his head. His voice grew serious. "Your parents, well, all of you were so involved in the Church." He looked away. "I also remember what brought your parents to their eternal rest. I still remember their funeral Mass. Half of Tyler must have shown up."

Paul froze, pivoting toward the bishop. He stepped back into the office. "Honestly, I don't remember much about their funeral."

Vance peered at him over his glasses. "Why did you become a priest, Paul?"

"I had the calling," Paul automatically replied.

Bishop Vance studied his younger priest and then nodded. He said, "The calling. Of course. Have a good day, Father."

***

Delia held a pair of faux sapphire teardrop earrings, considering if they were too extravagant for her date. Shaking her head, she murmured, "No," before dropping them back into her jewelry box. She reached for her small gold hoops, knowing they were a better fit for the likes of Paul Wainwright. Simple and understated.

The familiar pounding started as soon as she affixed her right earring.

"Oh shit. Why now?"

She descended her townhome's stairs, listening to the walls shake. Delia debated whether she should duck out the back, into the garage and bolt. History told her to take her chances and get this over with. It would be much easier than Frank hounding her for the next two days.

Spying her purse on the couch, she reached inside, grabbing her cell phone. Because her hands continued to shake, it took three attempts to turn it off. Searching for a sufficient hiding place, she opted to slide it as far under her couch as her fingers could reach.

When Frank's shouts of, "Delia, damn it!" grew louder, she decided she could stall no longer. Groaning, she flung open the door.

Hoping her face conveyed a pissed-off expression, she demanded, "It's nine in the morning. What the hell do you want?"

Frank stood, his arm stretched, blocking her way outside. "What do I want? I want you to tell me you're coming in today."

He didn't wait for an invitation to enter. In a single motion, he shoved past Delia. Plopping onto her couch, he propped his shoes on the beige ottoman while giving her the once-over. A lazy smile crossed his face. "You look damn hot for your day off. I always liked you in white."

"What's with you and my free time lately? I have a *job,* Frank. That means I go to work and do work things. And then when I come home, I do home things."

"We're short-staffed," Frank countered.

"The casino has plenty of staff for the Executive Concierge Desk. If you need more girls, go recruit. This isn't my problem."

Frank rose, strode over, and slid his arms around Delia, kissing her neck. He let his hand slip to her breast. "You're always my problem," he whispered. "We have a good thing, you and me."

Delia pushed him away. "Wrong. We aren't a 'thing.' We're done. Through. Find someone else." *Please!* Pointing toward the door, she added, "Leave."

"Did *you* find someone else? Is that why you're ducking away?"

"When would I have time to find someone else?" Delia asked. She rolled her eyes and put her hands on her hips. "Look, Mama's been sick. I'm on my way to visit her. Can we do this some other time? Seriously, Frank, I have a lot going on right now."

He grabbed her purse, flipped it upside down, and shook, eyeing the contents as they dropped to the ground. "What the hell are you doing?" Delia cried.

Grunting, he said, "Checking to see what you've got in here."

She threw up her hands, "Like what? Yellowcake uranium?"

Frank stopped, mid-shake. "What's that? Do you snort it or smoke it?"

Crouching, Delia gathered the items from her purse. "It isn't a drug."

"Don't see your phone," Frank commented.

"I left it at work. Stopping by the Dragon on my way out of town. Then I'm going by the deli, if you must know, and picking up some lunch for Mama."

"When are you back from Hickville?"

"I will be back from *Arkansas* Wednesday morning. Mama's an hour away. I'll be on time for my shift. Okay?"

Delia realized her voice might betray her at any moment. She also understood if she let Frank know he'd gotten the best of her, he'd stay, torment her, and keep her trapped. It turned him on to taunt her after he'd broken her down, stripping her to her most vulnerable. Already in her home, if he thought he'd won this round, history told her he'd stay anywhere from two hours to two days, showing her no mercy.

Putting the contents of her purse on the coffee table, she eyed Frank. Delia tossed her hair behind her shoulder while keeping her voice measured. "Look, Mama has a bunch of doctor's appointments in the next two days. I'm taking her to Texarkana. So, can we pick this up later? She doesn't know if the cancer's back."

When Frank said nothing, she added, "This has been going on for a while. I expect it will be going on for a longer while. I'd really appreciate it if you'd get off my back. Hire a few more girls. I need to focus on Mama. Tommy has weekends off. Maddy's got finals this week and summer school soon. So, I'm it for help."

Delia stopped, afraid she'd made her lie too specific. And more afraid God would punish her for maligning her mother's health. She waited, while offering a silent prayer Frank would extend her mercy.

"Didn't know. Sorry." He handed Delia her purse with enough force that she stepped backward to prevent herself from falling. As Frank twisted the doorknob, he called over his shoulder, "Give your mother my best. See you Wednesday."

Chapter Nine

The Inevitable Question

"I can't believe you've never been fishing," Paul said, baiting Delia's hook.

"I know! How did I get to be this old and miss all the excitement." Delia laughed.

Paul shook his head. "Don't tease."

"You're so cute when you pout. I'm having a great time, Mr. Wainwright. But I didn't know fishing would require me to impale worms. It seems inhumane." She nudged Paul with her shoulder.

He grinned, knowing he'd grown addicted to Delia's incidental touches. "I guarantee the worms don't suffer. Consider it part of God's Grand Design. Plus, it is a lot easier to eat a fresh fish dinner when you actually *catch* some fish."

"You mean we are going to eat these?" Delia asked. "I . . . well, confession here. I don't know how to cook."

"Could have fooled me." Paul winked as he picked up his sandwich off the ice chest. "If these didn't have a deli sticker on them, I'd have assumed they were homemade. Lucky for you, I do know how to cook fish. I can even teach you how to clean them." He stroked his chin. "How does that saying go? 'Clean a fish for a woman and she will eat for a day, teach a woman how to clean a fish and she can eat for a lifetime'?"

"My, my. You are certainly playful today, Mr. Wainwright," Delia said, batting her eyes. "Let me ask you, where did you go to college?"

Paul sat in his lawn chair, ankles crossed and enjoying the easy banter. A slight breeze kept the humidity at bay. He stole a glance in her direction.

"Ah, my illustrious academic career. I got my undergraduate in premed at the University of Arizona. Before my folks died, I wanted to be a doctor." He shrugged.

"I take it you have more than one degree?"

Paul swallowed a bite of his lunch, regretting the truth of his next statement. "I have a master's in clinical psychology and a master's in theology. Both from Notre Dame." He gulped. "The one in New Orleans." Paul eyed Delia, waiting for the next inevitable question.

She said, "Wow, no wonder you know so much. Explains why you are so religious too. I can see how that would make you such a great counselor."

Delia's fingers fluttered to Paul's arm. Regretting how much he'd soon miss her familiar warmth and the incredible sensation of her touch, he braced himself for her reaction to his upcoming betrayal. The thought of his shameful behavior hurting her stung worse than the idea that he would lose her friendship.

"Can I ask you something? I don't want to be rude."

He nodded, steadying his hand before taking a sip from his water bottle.

"Are you married?"

Liquid shot through Paul's nose as he began coughing. Delia stretched from her chair, patting his back. "No," he squeaked. "I'm definitely not married."

"Involved with someone?"

Paul shook his head. "Unattached. Married to my work. Truly."

"Just going to ask . . ."

"Not gay either, if that's what you were thinking."

"Glad to hear it. And yes."

He steadied himself, ready for what he expected to be the next question. Instead, Delia asked, "Any kids?"

Paul gazed across the water, avoiding Delia's eye. Nobody had ever asked him this question before, a byproduct of running away to the priesthood. The terrible coincidence tore through his heart: his freshly deceased parents were the first to meet his son.

The memory came flooding back, drowning him in the same sorrow that always swamped his emotions when he felt strong and distanced enough to reflect on that horrible week. Paul had been driving to his parents' funeral after he'd picked up Kayla from the airport. In an effort to find something—anything—positive in his grief and unanswered questions, he announced he wanted to name their baby after his father.

Kayla squeezed Paul's hand and then said, "It'll be a while. I took care of it."

Already numb from arriving at his parent's home a week earlier and discovering his father's bloody body, barely recognizable, and showing all the tell-tale signs of a terrible struggle, and then his mother's—oh what they'd done to his mother!—Paul didn't process Kayla's comment. "I'm glad you're here," he said, kissing her palm.

She tossed her head backward as her words kept coming. "I'm so glad you understand." Sighing, she said, "I know you said no before. But given what happened with your folks . . . I just . . . well, hell, Paul. Why put ourselves through this?"

He glanced at Kayla, and then swerved back into his lane, missing the oncoming car by mere feet. Paul unleashed his hand from hers, gripping the steering wheel with an unnatural strength. His voice trembling, he asked, "Put ourselves through *what*?"

Kayla placed her hand on her torso. "It wasn't like I was really showing." She rolled her eyes. "Dear God! I didn't look forward to getting fat."

The truck sped through Tyler in slow motion, with familiar landmarks of Paul's childhood now looking foreign and distorted. Kayla explained that while he dealt with his gristly discovery, she'd made some life decisions of her own.

"You were twenty-three weeks along!" he roared, letting the words echo through the truck's cab. When his breathing caught up with his thoughts, he added, "That was *our* son!"

Kayla kept her voice even, as if she were mollifying a petulant child. "You've been through a lot in the last few days." She rubbed his knee. "Look, right now, you don't know what you're saying. Paul, I know you. This is the grief of losing your parents talking. You don't need this. Besides, why should we be tied down by a screaming kid?"

When Paul stayed silent, she reached for his arm, giving him a gentle pat. "You'll be happy about this. Trust me."

That day, Paul sat in the pews next to Chuck and Allison. As the funeral progressed, he stared straight ahead at his parents' caskets, lost and numb. Only one thought played in his head. He no longer had a past, and Kayla took away his future.

The memory of that day ebbed out of his consciousness, leaving behind the void of heartache he knew so well. Raising his head, he saw Delia waiting for an answer. Paul looked out across the lake, watching the gentle movements of the water. He felt his eyes moisten but didn't touch his face for fear of giving in to his insurmountable grief.

His voice came out low and raspy. "Yes. One in Heaven."

"I'm so sorry. I can't imagine losing a child," Delia whispered.

Paul sat on the dock, making a point to count the flowers blooming on a distant magnolia tree, afraid to speak. Within seconds, he felt Delia standing next to him, her hands gliding across his shoulders, pulling him close. He relaxed, allowing his head to rest on her chest. She said nothing. Instead, she stroked his hair, as he mourned the loss of the son he never knew.

***

Two hours later, Paul hauled the ice chest with five catfish, two bass, and a crappie back to his truck. "You sure you don't want the alligator?"

"I like gators as much as snakes, thank you," Delia declared, shifting the fishing poles into her other hand. "He was a biggie. Besides, I suspect he wanted us more than we wanted him."

The alligator had reared his head under her pole just as Delia brought in her second bass. After a righteous scream, she declared, "We've caught enough fish today."

"I have a couple of errands to run," Paul said, as they reached his truck. "I can meet you at your house."

Delia stiffened her shoulders. Her face held an amused expression. "Oh? Fishing with anyone else today?"

"Hmmm, I hadn't thought about it, but yes, I suppose in a way, I am."

"I see," she said, pressing her lips together while her eyebrows formed a V above her nose.

Paul recognized the new playful and unfamiliar energy between them. However, there were his vows to think of. God wasn't a "yes-but" kind of Father. *All this can be avoided if you'd come clean.* He would tell her the truth, he resolved. But not today. Today, Delia offered him an indulgence of the very first comfort he'd received in fifteen years over the loss of his baby. He wanted to cherish this moment.

"You are more than welcome to come with me," Paul said. "I'm going to an assisted living facility and saying hello to a few homebound folks. I'm bringing Communion to them. I won't be too long. Maybe thirty minutes, an hour at the most."

"How can you do that?"

"Anyone in good standing with the Catholic Church can offer Communion. I'm sorry I didn't ask you. I guess I naturally assumed . . ."

"Sure. Sounds like fun," Delia said, tossing her hair behind her shoulder. "What? You seem surprised."

Paul shrugged. "I . . . I guess I didn't think it would be your thing."

"I'm not in 'good standing' as you say." Delia looked down, smoothing her skirt. "But, why not? I'd still like to come."

"My other errand is getting groceries so that we can cook a proper dinner. What kind of vegetable do you want with your catfish?"

"I'll go with you there too. That way I can pick the ice cream."

"Ice cream is not a vegetable."

"True," Delia said. "Okay, any vegetable but okra. That stuff's nasty and overrated."

Paul brought his fist to his chest. "You're breaking my heart. Okra is the national vegetable of Texas."

"And it can stay in Texas," Delia said.

****

Tuesday morning, Delia stopped by her downstairs hall mirror, pausing to fluff her hair. She checked her teeth to make sure they were free of lipstick. Passing inspection, she allowed herself to reenact last week's impromptu river walk dance, even going as far as to twirl, grab Paul's imaginary hand, and bow to the audience.

She let out a joyful giggle. Paul brought out the giddy teenager in her. The one Delia never had a chance to be. Three dates in, and for the first time in her life, she found herself infatuated with a man. Dark thoughts percolated in the recesses of her mind. If he only knew the truth. . .

The light tapping at Delia's door, a considerable change from Frank's pounding the day before, told Delia she had time for one more twirl. Saying a quick prayer, a practice she'd picked up recently, she thanked God for bringing Paul into her life.

If Delia had one complaint, it would be her frustration about Paul's romantic pace, or more to the point, the lack thereof. Because he had turned out to be nothing like any man she'd ever met, she made up her mind last night to let him set the speed for their physical interaction. She'd never met a man yet who didn't eventually come around. Even if he chose to be painstakingly slow, so be it.

Opening the door, she gazed at Paul. Today he wore a pair of jeans and a blue button-down shirt. She took a moment to admire his shoulders and then felt her cheeks grow hot when he noticed. His green eyes twinkled from behind his glasses. Delia drew her hand to her face in an effort to hide her embarrassment. "Good morning, Mr. Wainwright."

"For you," he said, handing her a bunch of daisies.

Holding the bouquet, Delia opened her mouth and closed it again. When no proper words came to mind, she repeated the action. Paul's simple gesture stunned her. It felt more personal than the baubles so many of her lonely clients bought her.

"Something wrong?"

Shaking her head, she motioned him inside. Finally figuring out the appropriate response, she said, "Thank you for the flowers. They are beautiful."

***

"Tell me," Paul said, rocking on his heels as they strolled through the Shreveport Aquarium, an hour later. "You heard my life story yesterday. Your turn."

Delia watched a school of jellyfish swim through the plexiglass tunnel. "Never married, unattached, straight, and no children that I know of."

"How come you never married?" He stepped back while raising his hands. "No. Sorry, I don't want to pry."

With a dismissive wave, Delia said, "I could ask the same of you. But for me, I had a long-term relationship. It didn't work out. We lived together for a few years. Nobody interesting after that."

"Same for me," Paul said.

"Ah." Delia nodded. "What did you do this morning?"

"Prepare to be bored." Paul raised two fingers. He touched his index finger. "I went to confession." He touched his middle finger. "And I went to Mass."

She sighed. "You are a good Catholic. An inspiration."

"That's the idea. Thank you."

Delia watched his cheeks grow red. She placed her fingers on his arm, then remembering her new vow to go at Paul's pace, drew her hand back. "I admire you for living your faith." She thought Paul's face changed to purple, or perhaps the dim light of the aquarium made his skin appear that way.

"Thank you," he muttered.

She put her hands behind her back, as a reminder not to reach for him. "Did you do anything else?"

"I went shopping at the St. Vincent dePaul thrift store and bought this shirt." He tugged on the collar, adding, "My other one smelled like last night's dinner."

Delia said, "Blue is certainly your color."

"If you didn't like it, I figured I'd give it to my brother."

"Oh, definitely keep the shirt," she said. This time she was certain the change in Paul's face wasn't from the aquarium lighting. "By the way, do you have a picture of this brother who looks like your twin?"

"Sure." Paul reached into his pocket. He twisted his mouth, pulling at his phone. "It's stuck. Just a sec." With one more yank, he released his cell. A string of beads followed behind, bouncing off every hard surface and rolling throughout the aquarium's floor.

"Oh dear!" Delia said, kneeling while helping Paul search for the tiny glass balls, which were now scattered around their feet. Thoughts of yesterday when Frank emptied the contents of her purse came to mind. "What was this?"

"Well, . . . Rats." Paul sighed. Delia suppressed a chuckle at his attempt at swearing. "It was my rosary."

She placed the beads she retrieved into his outstretched hand. "Sorry to hear that. Is it fixable?"

Paul shrugged. He eyed the remnants of his rosary and then crammed the loose beads into his pocket. "I can get another one." Swiping his phone screen, he passed it to her. "This is my brother, Chuck, and his wife, Brittany."

"Oh yes. I can definitely see what you mean by you being the better-looking brother." Delia nudged him, belatedly remembering she'd decided against physical contact.

Paul took a half-step closer in her direction. "And my sister and her sons." He pointed to his screen. "Garret's in the green shirt. The redhead is Archie, and the little one is Henry."

"Cute kids. I see the Wainwright resemblance in their faces. What about their father?"

"Allison's divorced. We tease her and tell her it's the only rule she's ever broken."

"That's too bad. Other pictures?" she asked, standing on her tiptoes as Paul moved the phone out of her reach.

He handed his cell back to her. "Here's one of me when we lost the basketball game."

Delia enlarged the photo, taking the time to check out Paul's legs. "I see you were playing at a church," she said.

"Why . . . why do you say that?" Paul stammered.

"Well, look at the people in the stands." She pointed to the audience. "Either that or a lot of priests like basketball."

Chapter Ten

The Problem

"Tell me," Tawana said, sipping her latte after she and Delia found a seat at their favorite coffee shop. "You've been in a happy mood lately. That South American guy in room 1209 was good for your ego."

"Nah, Mr. Gonzales was a perfect gentleman. He just wanted someone to go out with every night. Told me all about his wife," Delia said, dabbing her lips. She placed her napkin next to her drink and then leaned forward, propping her chin in her hands. "I met someone."

Tawana's eyebrows rose. "Oh? Do tell?"

Delia looked away, aware of the flush spreading across her face. In the past several weeks, she hadn't found a precise way to describe Paul. "He's a different kind of man than what you'd find at the Dragon."

"I see. You mean 'different' as in decent and respectable." Tawana asked, "Does Frank know?"

"No. He's suspicious. God may strike me down for this. I told him Mama's sick again. It was the only way he'd stop hounding me."

"You and Frank . . ." Tawana shook her head. "Well, it isn't my business."

"It isn't that simple, T," Delia murmured, studying her hands.

"I believe it *is* that simple. You have a job. Frank has a job. You keep saying it's over, but not acting like it's over."

Delia rolled her eyes. "It's officially over. I mean, I'd like to think that's the case."

"Was Frank this possessive when you were together?"

"Worse." She slumped in her chair. "I know Frank's bad for me. He's mean. He's controlling . . ." She twisted her fingers. "He's just . . ." She let the words hang.

"It's an abusive relationship, Delia," Tawana stated. "Abigail and I have watched you guys for years. I'd have cut off his balls the first time his fist came near me."

Delia concentrated on a hairline crack in the table, wishing her friend would stop staring. "I know. Frank came by two nights ago."

She shuddered as she recalled how Frank showed up drunk on her doorstep. He pestered her, backing her into a corner, helping himself. After a drawn-out cat-and-mouse game, Delia brought him upstairs to get it over with, hoping she gave him enough to appease him.

Instead, Frank dug in, tearing down her fragile self-esteem. "You're damn lucky I came along, or you'd still be waiting tables. Or worse, you'd only be a two-bit whore, back in Hickville, living in a single-wide with six kids and no baby daddy. Just like your mother," he said as he lay on top of her. "You're too stupid for anything else." Delia heard his words so many times she believed them.

Tawana sighed. "Of course, once Frank starts going down this road with you, we all suffer." She shook her head. "It's hard on all of us that you and our boss are an on-again, off-again thing. No wonder Frank has been an ass to everyone lately."

"Frank was born an ass," Delia grumbled. "I wish he'd go away."

"Honey, the only way Frank will go away is if you quit your job." Tawana eyed her. "Are you ready to quit the Dragon?"

"I finally paid off Mama's medical bills. Her cancer's been gone three years," she whispered. "Now I want to see Maddy graduate from college. I swear, I'm quitting the day Maddy has her diploma. Then I'm getting as far from the Dragon as possible."

"I know you will. When you're ready. It's true for all of us." Tawana patted her friend's hand. "In the meantime, . . ."

"In the meantime, the money and the perks are good. Did I tell you I paid off the townhouse last year?"

Tawana raised her eyebrows. "Good for you."

"Do you know Cedric Lennox? He works at Shreveport Investments? He's a regular at the Dragon."

"I believe I do." Tawana chuckled. "Intimately."

Delia leaned forward. "He's handling my portfolio. I'm doing well. I'm thinking about my future. I'm thinking about my family too. Maddy has one more year of college. She has a scholarship, but I'm paying for her housing expenses."

"I should call Cedric." Tawana sighed. She sat back in her chair. "So, let's hear about the mystery man."

Delia took her time, savoring every sweet memory. "It's been casual. I've never met someone like him. He's so . . ." Her hand flew into the air, grasping for the proper description. "Genuine. Paul, that's his name. He lives in Ballentine, Texas, about seventy miles from here. South of Tyler. He's a counselor at a prison."

"Go on." Tawana nodded.

"Very tall. Smart too." She leaned forward. "Paul has two master's degrees. One in psychology and the other in . . . Oh, what was it? Something to do with religions."

"Wow. I'll bet there's a great backstory there." Tawana rubbed her hands together. "Let's hear what's making you smile like I've never seen you smile before."

"We've been seeing each other for about a month and a half. Sometimes he comes to Shreveport for the day, sometimes two days. This past week, he and his brother went to Dallas for some sort of big basketball game. His favorite team is in the playoffs. You know I don't keep up with sports." She rumpled her face. "Anyway, I met Paul Friday night for a late dinner in a little town about thirty minutes from here on the other side of the state line."

Tawana shook her head. "I can't believe you took a Friday night off. Well, it explains why Frank barreled through the Dragon's halls, demanding to know where you were. He's gonna track your car if you aren't careful."

"He already has. When Frank came over this week, he asked why I'd been in Texas." Delia ran her hands through her hair before turning toward her friend. "I've already called the dealership. I'm buying another car tomorrow—one Frank won't know about. I'll keep the Honda and use it to drive to work."

"So, have you gone to visit your Mr. Paul?" Tawana asked.

"I've offered." She tilted one shoulder. "Honestly, it's a little frustrating. I don't want him to think he has to do all the driving. But Paul keeps saying there's nothing to do in Ballentine." She scoffed. "As if Shreveport is the South's Excitement Central."

Tawana sipped her drink. Peering over the coffee cup, she said, "It seems to me, you of all people, particularly with your specialized expertise, could think of *something* to do."

Delia straightened her napkin, taking her time to make it parallel with the table's side before she spoke. She muttered, "Nothing has happened with Paul. No hugging, or anything else one might consider in my line of 'specialized expertise.'"

"A true gentleman or gay?"

"Definitely a gentleman. And definitely not gay," Delia said.

Tawana lowered her eyes. "And where does he stay when he comes to town if nothing is happening?"

"He never asks to sleep at my place. Paul says he knows people in Shreveport from his job who have extra rooms. He said they don't mind him staying with them."

"What about putting him at the Dragon?"

"Oh, hell no!" Delia said.

Tawana let out a deep laugh. "So, your new friend doesn't know what you do?"

"He knows I work in customer relations."

"That's one way to put it," Tawana said. "Personally, I've always had a tough time having long-term boyfriends, given what I do for a living. How have you made out?"

"Frank's been the only boyfriend," Delia said.

"How do you think Paul's going to take it when he's ready for your brand of affection and finds out you are selling it the other five nights a week?"

Delia groaned. She hung her head, rolled her shoulders, and eyed Tawana. "Don't you think I've thought about that? Besides, I can't quit my job after knowing a guy six weeks. But it's a problem. If not Paul, it'll be the next man."

"Preach, girlfriend. I live this too."

She leaned forward. "Seriously, T. I'm embarrassed. Most people don't have this kind of job. And I don't like to think about it. Otherwise, I start feeling guilty. How will I ever be able to explain what I do? To my family? To anyone?" She threw up her hands. "But what else am I qualified to do? I should have run back to Lewisville years ago, instead of hooking up with Frank. But I didn't want to face it then. I don't want to face it now. And it isn't just the job. Who would want me if they knew? Knew about who—what I am?"

"I have no answers. I'm living this as well."

Delia splayed her fingers on the table and let out a soft giggle. "I gotta tell you I really like Paul."

"Even though you aren't getting any from him?"

"I'm in no hurry if he isn't." She smiled. "It's romantic. Paul always asks about my week. Like he's genuinely interested in me. He doesn't swear. He won't watch an R movie—says it is the principal of the thing. He insists on paying when we go out, but I don't think he makes nearly as much as I do. I can tell by the way he dresses and what he orders. Sometimes we share the meal." She curled her nose and said, "Not like the high roller clients at the Dragon who are offended if I don't order lobster."

Delia continued, "A few weeks ago, he took me to the aquarium. Did I mention he's Catholic? He had a rosary with him. It broke and the beads rolled everywhere." Reaching into her bag, she said, "Anyway, I stopped by this little Catholic shop today and I picked up this." She held a blue, ornately beaded rosary between her fingers. "I hope he likes it."

"It's like you're in high school, going steady," Tawana said.

"The boys I knew in high school didn't 'go steady.' I guess that's why I like Paul so much. He isn't asking anything of me. He likes me for who I am."

"Every girl's dream," Tawana said.

Delia sipped her latte. "I've been thinking about asking him if he wants to go with me to see Mama. I don't want to make Paul feel like he has to. But, well, I don't know." She looked at Tawana. "Do you think it'd send the wrong message?"

"What message exactly?"

Grinning, she said, "I guess that I think he's special."

***

Delia must be busy this week, Paul thought, as he drove to Ballentine Correctional Thursday. He shook his head, wishing that the act cleared his thoughts. Paul knew he needed to stop thinking about her. As much as he always enjoyed their time together, it was obvious Delia regarded him as nothing more than a platonic friend. However, he had a problem.

Guilt from his own deception weighed on him. It wasn't just the fact Paul still hadn't told Delia he was a priest, something he promised himself he would do when the next opportunity presented itself. Paul groaned, shaking his head again. He didn't need an extra serving of regret. *Especially* today.

Paul tapped the steering wheel while the miles on the two-lane Texas highway ticked by. In the last six days, he'd kept to himself, brooding, yet wanting to reach out to Delia. However, he recognized the need to stay true to his vows. Penance, Paul decided last week, for not keeping his personal feelings in check.

"She's probably busy," he mumbled.

After parking, Paul checked into the guard station, just like he did every visit. This week, though, his heart filled with dread. He'd arrived an hour earlier to take care of his frustrating errand.

As Paul gave his credentials to the guard, his phone pinged. "Just wanted to say hi." Delia wrote.

Paul read the message twice, enjoying her five words. A gift from Above! How else could he describe being in such a miserable place, with the daunting task in front of him, and then receiving Delia's message at that exact moment?

With his spirits lifted, he replied, "Hi. How's your week going?" before stashing his phone and his keys into the tattered briefcase Ally gave him when he started graduate school.

From somewhere in the halls, Paul heard men's voices yelling, followed by the sound of swearing. In the distance a buzzer sounded, breaking the spell Delia's text cast over him.

"Christ's peace be with you," Paul said to the guards, offering them a blessing, as he stepped into the prison.

Even though two months passed since the riot, his enthusiasm for his ministry had not returned. Paul continued praying for direction, not ready to let it go. In the back of his mind, he knew he'd failed Armetta. He'd failed Foster, too—if he wanted to be completely truthful. Marvin Foster may have convinced himself and his mother of his absolution, but Paul held no such notion about his own soul. He hoped Foster would offer enough grace to allow him to process his own pain.

"What can I do for you, Father?" Marvin asked when they were seated in the visitor's room. The guard stood in the corner, throwing out an intimidating look. Paul figured if a fight broke out among the three of them, he and the guard stood less than half a chance. Foster knew it.

He handed him a Snickers candy bar, contraband in Shackleford's anti-outside food policy. The guard acknowledged Paul's transgression and shrugged it off. "Thanks," Foster said, unwrapping it. "Must be a biggie for you to come all the way here with candy."

"How are you doing these days?" Paul asked.

Foster shrugged. "Armetta's gone. Trial ain't gonna be pretty. Self-defense, you know?"

"I need a favor from you, Marvin," Paul said, keeping his voice even and focusing on doing the same with his facial features.

"Whatcha need?"

"Confessions are bound to secrecy. I cannot share what you told me with anyone without your permission."

Foster suppressed a laugh. "I'm not stupid. That's why I asked for you that night."

"Marvin, please. Hear me out." Paul waited a beat. "With your permission, I'd like to share your confession with one person and one person only."

"You telling me you want me to give you permission to rat me out to someone? You're crazy, Father," Foster said, reclining in his chair. The candy wrapper now dangling from his meaty index finger. "There's no amount of chocolate you can bring me to make me do that."

Though he expected this, Foster's lack of cooperation still landed like a punch in the gut. Paul sat straighter now. "Marvin, I'd like to discuss what happened that night from *my* perspective with someone. My sister is a licensed therapist. She's bound by the State of Texas for confidentiality as well. I'd like to talk to her. Nobody else. Not lawyers. Not Shackleford. Just her."

He fixed his glare on Paul. "I don't know your sister." Foster crossed his arms, adding, "If it really is your so-called 'sister.' I didn't make a confession to your sister. I made it to you." He uncrossed his arms and leaned forward. "You can't say a damn thing. It was self-defense. You did your job that night. God and I are now square. Appreciate it. The rest ain't your business."

Paul hesitated before replying. "Confession doesn't work that way, Marvin. You made a choice. God gives us free will. You had options."

Foster snorted. "I don't know what you're talking about. It was self-defense. That's what my lawyer says. No witnesses." His voice now took on a menacing tone as he moved toward Paul. "And no. Don't get any ideas. You ain't discussing this with anyone."

After their meeting, Foster sat in Paul's ministry hour. To drive his message home, he brought three of his biggest and most disruptive friends with him. The four caused enough chaos to make the other prisoners leave, one by one during the service. In the end, the guards escorted Foster and his buddies out of the prison's chapel, but not without Foster and his thugs casting warning glares in Paul's direction as they exited.

With his afternoon at Ballentine Correctional finally finished, Paul sat in his truck, rubbing his temples. Ally's words replayed in his head: *"Maybe you've outgrown that season of your life?"*

Images of his parents came to his mind. "Nope." Paul sighed. "Still my season."

Opening his briefcase, he pulled out his keys and phone. A smile grew when he saw Delia had replied. "Worked all week. What about you, stranger? Let me know when you're coming back to Shreveport."

He hovered his hand over his cell, wondering how best to reply. *It will be a few weeks?* Or, *I'm not sure, I'll let you know?* But, Paul reasoned, how was putting Delia off being fair to her? She didn't have an attraction problem. He did.

"I'm free Monday and Tuesday. What about you?" he replied.

Chapter Eleven

The Denial

Monday morning, Paul, with his rosary draped through his fingers, sat in the parking lot of Our Lady of the Lake, a small Catholic church just inside the Louisiana state line. His dashboard clock told him he had another eight minutes before the church doors unlocked for the day.

Conscious of his truck's Texas license plates, Paul lowered his Rangers cap over his eyes, without letting go of the rosary. The memory of Delia's present returned to him, bringing a lazy smile to his face.

She'd greeted him at the door of her townhouse. "Here. This is for you," she said, thrusting a gift bag at him.

"Me?" Paul asked. "You didn't have to."

Delia leaned into his shoulder, bumping him, bringing with her touch that same sensation Paul craved. "I know, but I wanted to. I thought, well, I don't know," she stammered as he watched her blush.

He opened the bag, stunned at her thoughtfulness. "Thank you," he said, hoping his gratitude came through in those two simple words.

"I . . . well, I don't really know what you do with this. You pray with it right?" Delia asked.

"Sort of. The rosary is used for a Scripture-based prayer about Christ's life." Paul sat on her couch, examining the exquisite beadwork. Delia slid next to him. Looking at her, he said, "Let me teach you the prayers."

She nodded.

Taking her hand, he led it to the silver cross. The familiar tingle of her flesh flew up his arm, a feeling he treasured. "We start here," he said, looking into her eyes as they made the sign of the cross together.

While Paul replayed the memory, he allowed himself a moment alone with the indulgence of his thoughts, while ignoring the oppressive guilt stemming from his attraction. When the heaviness won out, he left his truck, in search of redemption.

As he walked into the tiny church, he noticed the shine reflecting off the wood floors in the vestibule. Polished floors, a small detail, but one he wished Saint Daniel's adopted. Straightening his Rangers cap, Paul debated the etiquette of wearing a hat in church versus taking a chance someone might recognize him, even though he was one state and more than an hour away from home.

Entering the main chapel, he admired the stained glass with the morning's rays breaking through and leaving deep reds and blues on the opposing walls. Paul added envy to his mental list of sins, noting how the Diocese of Shreveport was more willing to invest in modern, attractive churches in small towns—which would bring in more parishioners—than Bishop Vance. He inhaled, surprised to discover the stale, mildewed carpet smell he was used to at Saint Daniel's replaced by the pleasant aroma of cedar, another small but significant detail to give the congregation a sense of ownership in their parish.

Dipping his fingers into the holy water font, Paul crossed himself. Finding a suitable pew near the confessional, he genuflected toward the

Tabernacle, noting the ornate altar. Another covetous sin to add to his growing list. He gave a solemn nod toward a couple of faithful Catholics, waiting for their confession before morning Mass.

When his turn came, Paul secured the wooden confessional door, listening to the latch click behind him. The voice behind the wooden screen said, "In the name of the Father, the Son, and the Holy Spirit."

Through seven years of muscle memory, Paul caught himself before he uttered the same words and made the sign of the cross. Regaining his composure, he said, "Bless me, Father, for I have sinned," as he folded his lanky frame to a kneeling position in the cramped confessional. Relieved to have a screen between him and the anonymous priest, he snatched his hat from his head, scrunching into his hand while letting out a deep exhale. "It has been about a month since my last confession."

"How can I help you?" came the subdued voice from the other side of the screen.

As many times as Paul said the same phrase under similar circumstances, he froze at hearing those words. Closing his eyes, he flexed his hands, replaying the priest's voice, wondering if he'd ever met this man. Though confessions were bound to silence, he didn't need a well-meaning member of the clergy—one of his own—taking him aside, thinking they were helping him stay accountable to his priestly vows.

The same calm voice behind the screen added, "Whenever you are ready."

Paul relaxed his shoulders, confident of his anonymity. He imagined the priest glancing at his watch, knowing he had to start Mass shortly. "Sorry . . . sorry for making you wait."

"Quite all right."

"Thank you." A smile formed on Paul's lips, wondering if the man on the other side of the screen would count that as a lie when he went to his own confession. "Father, I find that even today I am suffering from envy. Envy that others have better resources in their jobs than I do. I recognize my lack of gratitude and my frustration at not being heard by my coworkers is causing resentment. Therefore, I find that I'm distracted. I'm not doing my best in my job."

"Thank you for sharing this. Is that all?"

"I recognize that I am making decisions which are against the long-term choices I've already made." Paul cringed, listening to his empty words, which carried no weight.

The priest apparently agreed, asking, "Such as?"

Paul shifted on the kneeler. "Specifically, I am having inappropriate thoughts and strong physical desires for a woman whom I am not married to, nor see any future with," he blurted. "And because of these thoughts, I find that I am making excuses to others so I can be around her. I am not lying to those in my life, it is more like I am omitting important facts."

"Have you acted upon your feelings?"

Paul shook his head, as if the other priest could see him. "No."

"This woman," the priest started, "does she feel the same way about you?"

He shook his head again. Belatedly he added, "No. Not that I can tell."

A heavy sigh came from the other side of the confessional screen. "Thank you for staying true to your faith. I commend you for not acting on your thoughts. Especially as this woman is not your wife. Continue to not act upon your feelings. If you are tempted, distract yourself. Read Matthew Chapter 5."

"'But I say to you, everyone who looks at a woman with lust has already committed adultery with her in his heart,'" Paul stated.

"Exactly. It sounds like you are familiar with that particular verse." The priest continued, "Some people think lust stems from selfishness or lack of self-control. No. It stems from a void. An emptiness."

Paul tilted his head. "I . . . I guess I hadn't thought of it like that."

"Is there anything else you need to confess?"

"I . . ." He leaned back, resting on his heels while he gripped his hands behind his neck. Familiar feelings from the past few months bubbled to the surface. He felt the weight in his chest grow heavier as he thought of Marvin Foster. "I have become discouraged. Anxious. I've allowed an incident last spring to consume my thoughts. Though I thought I'd forgiven the person who caused the issue, the truth is, I've harbored resentment." He knelt straighter, resting his hands on the shelf in the middle of the screen. "Sometimes I think I hold on to the resentment because it is easier than looking at the bigger areas in my life where I've lost my way."

A chuckle came from the other side of the wooden screen. "How is that working out for you?"

Paul gave a light laugh in return. "About as well as can be expected." He considered his words as he continued. "The person I've been angry with represents a path I believe I've been led to rectify in my life. It just seems like maybe . . ."

"Maybe that's not your path?"

"It *is* my path. My only choice," Paul said, his voice braced with authority. Before the priest could respond, he added, already feeling the heaviness lift from his heart, "Oh yes. I have another sin I need to repent.

A couple of weeks ago, I gossiped to a friend, making light of my sister's divorce. For these sins, I am truly sorry."

"For your penance, you will forgive this person who wronged you."

"I will, Father," Paul mumbled. *At some point.* Ready to be done with his confession, he recited the Act of Contrition.

"That was good. It sounds like you have the Act of Contrition prayer down. Most people don't."

"Practice." Paul stood, unfolding his limbs. He arranged his hat onto his head.

"We should all practice," the priest commented.

By the time the priest finished his last prayer and gave absolution, Paul rested his hand on the confessional door. "Amen," Paul said, hastily making the sign of the cross. "Thank you, Father." As he left the church, his redemption from his confession grew, renewing his spirit and resolving to keep his thoughts of Delia and their friendship platonic.

Paul jumped into his truck and turned over the engine, grateful for the air conditioning, which seemed to be working overtime dissipating the summer's humidity. He adjusted his glasses while muttering, "She's just a friend. I am stronger than this."

Turning out of the parking lot toward Shreveport, Paul felt the guilt from his unrequited feelings for Delia fluttering away like a butterfly with new wings. However, experience from the past few weeks told him he needed more than a mere confession to keep his feelings at bay.

"Please help me so I can help myself," he prayed, wondering what he could do as additional penance when his mind drifted into his desires for Delia.

Paul's phone rang as he crossed into Shreveport's city limits. He answered through his truck's hand's free connection. "Good morning,

Father Wainwright, it's Father LeBlanc at All Saints. How are you this morning?"

"I'm good, Sir," Paul replied. "Is there no room in the inn tonight?"

"Oh, we have plenty of room for you. What I was wondering is if you'd be willing to help us out on Tuesday morning. We have a funeral Mass at ten. The mayor passed away. Expecting a big crowd. Could you help me officiate and serve Communion?"

Paul calculated if he and Delia had any concrete plans on Tuesday. Nothing specific had been set, other than the expectation they'd see each other both days before he headed back to Ballentine.

Paul said, "It isn't a problem. However, I don't have my priest vestments with me."

"Got you covered. Thank you for the help."

"Thank you for the place to stay tonight," Paul said, pleased to have his prayer answered as well as another way to atone.

***

"I thought you were spending the day with your man?" Tawana asked Tuesday morning while sliding into Delia's new Toyota Camry.

"Don't I wish." Delia smoothed her black skirt. "Duty calls." She turned onto Interstate 49 toward All Saints Catholic Church. "It worked out. He said he had something to do. Work stuff. A meeting or something this morning."

"This is 'work stuff' too."

"Not anymore." Delia giggled.

"True. May our dear mayor rest in peace," Tawana said, flipping him off. "Asshole."

"I'm sure that's how his wife feels," Delia said. "Think she'll know who we are?"

Tawana shrugged. "We are two of many. Plus, I doubt she cares at this point. Today we are concerned citizens, paying our last respects." She placed her hand on her heart and continued, "And as an added bonus, we are keeping Frank off our asses by acting as representatives of the Dragon."

"I'm sick of Frank," Delia grumbled, gripping the steering wheel tighter.

"He hit you again, didn't he?"

She stared straight ahead.

"Come on Delia, I saw the bruises on your shoulder. What'd you tell Paul?"

"Paul doesn't know," she whispered. "He hasn't seen them."

Tawana shook her head. "Why do you let Frank push you around?"

She didn't answer, instead concentrating on the heavy traffic at her exit ramp on their way to the church.

"This Paul guy?" Tawana started. "Why does he go back to Texas? Married? Is he telling his wife he has to work in Louisiana two days a week?"

"I don't think so. I asked him. He said he's been married to his work for years." Delia looked at her friend. "I believe him."

"So, what's his long-term plan? I mean, have you guys talked about a future?"

"It's only been a few months." She sighed. "Besides, I don't know what *my* future is. What do I say to him? I'm a high-end call girl with an asshole ex-boyfriend who is also my boss and I suppose would be considered my pimp? I mean, come on, T, that's pretty much what it boils down to. I'm damaged goods. He's too good for me. Paul wouldn't want me if he knew."

"Paul doesn't seem to 'want' you now."

"*I know!*" Delia slammed her hand into the steering wheel.

"Sorry," Tawana said, "didn't mean to hit a nerve."

She shook her head. "No. I'm fine. I guess I'm just confused. But I kind of like it, too." Delia turned her head to look at her friend. A smile crossed her face. "It might sound corny, you know, the kind of thing you hear in old movies, T. But honestly, I like that Paul's been a gentleman. But at the same time, yeah, I wonder what's wrong with me that he won't make a move. You know he still hasn't kissed me? I mean, we haven't talked about it or anything. I'm afraid to bring it up. I'm used to a different kind of dating, I guess."

"You are used to married men and Frank. We both are." Tawana sighed. "What you have is something special."

"Exactly. And I don't want to spoil that. When Paul's ready, I'll be ready. Hell, I'm more than ready."

"I'm totally jealous," Tawana said.

"You know what else?" Delia offered. "I haven't told him this, but I've been going to church."

"No kidding?"

"That's what pissed off Frank. That of all things. When he found out I didn't answer my phone last Sunday morning because I was at Mass, he lost it. I've been going for the past few weeks. Church, God, that kind of thing's important to Paul. So, I thought I'd start going. Maybe I'll tell him at some point. Right now, I'm going for myself."

"Really?" Tawana didn't hide the astonishment in her voice. "You never do anything for yourself."

"Maybe it's time I change that," Delia said, pulling into the church parking lot. She looked around at the crowd gathering toward the front. "This place is packed."

"We're going to be walking pretty far. In this heat and in these heels, too."

"Screw it, T. Let's get out of here. I'm sick of this."

"Are you sure? Frank won't be happy."

"I don't give two shits if Frank is happy. I'm sick of Frank. I'm sick of the Dragon. I'm sick of my job. Let's get breakfast."

***

Paul whistled as he walked through the rectory's kitchen late Tuesday night. He shifted his duffle bag to his left hand and whipped his phone out of his back pocket. Pausing at the staircase, he sent Delia a short text, as he promised, letting her know he'd arrived home. Her response, "Glad to hear it. It was fun!" made him smile. The following picture she included of the two of them at the hardware store, with Delia holding up a skill saw as she shopped for a birthday gift for her brother. Her caption: "I never knew power tools could be glamorous," caused him to chuckle.

He placed his leg on the stair tread, ready to reply when he heard the sound of a gentle cough coming from the living room. "Paul, if you have a moment." He froze in mid-step. Costa said, "I have something I'd really like to talk to you about."

In a covert move, Paul tucked his phone into his pocket as he turned toward Costa. Swallowing, he said, "Sir, it's after eleven. Would it be okay to talk in the morning?"

Costa offered a smile as he shook his head. "Now is much better." He pointed toward the couch next to him. "Please Paul, come sit."

Paul held up his duffle, stalling as he fumbled through his vocabulary. "Sir, if you don't mind, I'd like to put this away. Let me . . . I'll be right back." Before Costa could reply, Paul sped up the staircase. In his room, he shut his door while his heart raced. Fleeting muscle memories of high school, sitting in Costa's office, ready to be scolded for some earned transgression floated through his memories. What caused these feelings now, he wondered.

"Oh no," he grumbled as the realization dawned, doing nothing to slow his heart rate. *Paul.* Costa called him Paul instead of Father Wainwright.

Dumping his bag on his bed, he paced the room. "Lord, please . . ." he asked, unsure of what his prayer needed to be.

After ensuring his emotions wouldn't betray him, Paul returned to the living room. Costa looked up from his crossword. He asked, "What's a four-letter word for bone? Ends with an A?"

"Ulna, Sir," Paul said, as he positioned himself on the rectory's ancient couch.

"Oh, yes. Thank you." He scratched the word into his puzzle. "That works."

"You wanted to see me?"

Costa set his puzzle aside. "You've been with us for, what, six years?"

"Seven, actually." Paul crossed his legs.

Costa picked up his pencil, running it between his fingers. "The prison ministry? Word on the street is you are doing a great job. How do you feel that is going?"

Paul uncrossed his legs. "To my knowledge, very well. I have a couple of men in there who have asked the warden to start a Bible study. Hopefully that will happen in the next week. I meet with some of the inmates and provide counseling as well as hearing confessions before Mass on Thursdays." He drew in a breath while eyeing Costa. "Any complaints?"

Monsignor Costa raised his palms upward. "Not that I know of. The warden tells me your ministry is taking off. He mentioned he was grateful for what you did last April."

"Thank you, Sir." Paul strummed his fingers on his leg. He pressed his lips together, counting backward from five before he asked, "Is that what you wanted to know?" He began to rise. "It's late. I really need to get some sleep. I'm conducting Mass in the morning."

"Please sit, Paul." Costa set the pencil aside again. He reached for his water glass. Changing his mind, Costa grabbed the pencil once more. "I have another issue I'd like to discuss. I'm hoping perhaps you could help me. I spoke with Father LeBlanc at All Saints in Shreveport. He called, thanking me for your assistance with that funeral Mass."

Paul shifted, hoping to hide his astonishment. "It wasn't a problem." He kept his voice measured, adding. "I was happy to help."

Costa eyed him. "He said you didn't have your vestments?"

"I forgot them," Paul said, his voice dry.

"Strange." Monsignor eyed him. "As priests, we know to carry our vestments. Or, at least our stole. Do you not have an extra one in your truck?"

"I'm sorry, Sir. I took it out when I cleaned my truck a couple of weeks ago." Paul gave a small, conciliatory smile. "I forgot to put it back in. Obviously, yesterday was an important reminder."

"Agreed." Monsignor Costa pushed his lips together. He tapped his fingers. "Father LeBlanc tells me you spend a bit of time there."

Forgetting a stole didn't measure up to his teenage antics, but Paul didn't want to disappoint him any more now than he did when he was sixteen. He swallowed. "What exactly is it you want to know, Sir?"

The monsignor let out a breath, dropping his shoulders. "Obviously your time off is your own time. We are fortunate to have three priests at our small parish. Part of that is because of favors I called in from the bishop. Never mind that . . ." Costa's hand cut through the air. "You are well loved by the parishioners. You are invaluable in the community. The money you raised from the basketball tournament gave publicity to a great cause. And, as you just said, the prison ministry you started is thriving."

"Thank you, Sir." Paul yawned as he rose. "If that'll be all . . ."

Costa put his hands up while jutting his chin. "Look. I was a young man once. I realize there are temptations in the world. Is there anything you need to confess?"

Paul froze halfway between sitting and standing. "I don't believe there is." He shook his head. "No. Definitely not." Taking his time, he lowered himself onto the couch once more before he asked, "Why?"

"Paul." The monsignor peered over his glasses. "There are a lot of casinos in Shreveport. You are spending a great deal of time away from our parish on your days off. If I were to call other parishes in Shreveport, would I find out you had been bunking there as well?"

Costa didn't wait for an answer. "Gambling is not something to be taken lightly. If you have a problem, if you need to seek guidance, or if you need help with—dare I say—a gambling addiction, I'm here. As your friend. As your confidant. As your confessor.

"I've known you all your life. You are a good man, but even good men are tempted, Son. You are entrusted with Church money, and I wouldn't want a dark mark on Saint Daniel's if money were to be missing because it was being misused in a casino."

Paul raised an eyebrow as his heartbeat slowed back to normal. "*Is* money missing?"

He shook his head. "Not to my knowledge."

"That's good," Paul said, rising a third time. "Thank you, Sir. I assure you, I don't gamble. There is no need to be concerned."

"Is there any reason why you go away every week?" Costa blurted.

Paul gave his mentor a reassuring smile, taking his time searching for the right words. "Sir, I am in a state of grace. I take my vows seriously. I'm not gambling. I leave town on my days off to refresh and rejuvenate. Sometimes I visit the hospitals and homeless shelters as a member of the clergy. I help out at All Saints as well. I come back to Saint Daniel's a new man, full of Christ's Peace. Thank you for your concern. I'm sorry if I've given you or Father Morales any cause for worry. If that's the case, I will do better in the future," he added with sincerity in his voice. "Please believe me when I say, I'm touched and humbled that you wanted to speak with me. Rest assured, my priorities are in order. And I'll also put my extra stole back in my truck first thing in the morning."

"It sounds like it is me who needs to apologize." Costa sighed. "Father Wainwright, please forgive me. I guess I thought the worst. We priests are also flesh and blood."

Chapter Twelve

The Uncomfortable Truth

"I'm glad you were able to take an afternoon off and meet me. My work was slow today," Delia started as she and Paul walked along the streets of Jefferson Texas, Saturday afternoon. She hesitated, "Paul, I have a question. Why are you so mysterious about Ballentine?"

She nudged his shoulder, making his ice cream careen off course and land on his cheek instead of in his mouth. Delia's fingers floated to Paul's face, wiping away the chocolate. "There. All clean. Sorry about that."

Paul licked his cone, stalling, while calculating the best way to answer her question. He averted his gaze away from her legs, which were peeking out from under her purple and white floral skirt, with another new resolve to stay true to his vows. He'd read the Book of Matthew enough for one week.

Raising an eyebrow, he asked, "Mysterious?"

"Okay, pick your description, Mr. Wainwright." Delia grinned, nudging him again. "But we've both been busy with work this week, and I hate that you always do the driving. Like I've told you before, I'm more than happy to come your direction."

"Jefferson is nice. About halfway. A touristy kind of place, don't you think?"

"Yes, I do. I love this little town, but you aren't answering my question."

"Well, let's see. There's nothing to—"

She waved her hand. "I know, I know. There's nothing to do in Ballentine. But you've told me about the Wagon Wheel's chicken fried steak. I could come for lunch sometime."

"Is there a reason you'd want to go all that way?" Paul asked, using his forearm to wipe away the sweat on his brow.

"I want to be fair. You do all the driving. I don't mind, you know." Delia sighed. She tugged Paul's arm, lowering him to the red wooden bench outside an antique shop. "Sit with me. Tell me what you are afraid to tell me. You are married? You are living with someone? Why don't you want me to show up in Ballentine?"

Paul tossed the remainder of his cone in the nearby trashcan, pleased he'd made the shot. "You are correct, Miss Hargrove," he winked. "I am living with someone. Actually, I live with two someones."

Delia's face paled.

"No! I don't mean it like that," he said.

This time he nudged her and she giggled.

"I have two roommates. Walter and Alejandro. We live in a small house, built seventy years ago. It's nestled between the Wagon Wheel and the local Catholic Church."

Delia peered into Paul's phone at the picture of the yellow clapboard house he showed her. "My room's the second one from the left," he said, pointing at the small window on the top floor. "I've known Walter since I was a kid. He's in his 70s now. In fact, he was my high school principal and mentor. As a teenager, I looked for trouble. One time I even ran away and lived with him for a week after I got into a fight with my father."

"I have a hard time believing you were a rebel."

"Well, when you have a twin who doesn't break the rules, I think there's a natural tendency to want to test the system," Paul said.

"So, what happened?" Delia asked.

Paul grinned. "I should back up. I mentioned I've known Walter all my life because my mom taught at the same high school where he worked. My father grew up with him in Tyler, so they'd been friends since they were kids. Walter played basketball himself. He coached mine and my brother's teams when we were kids."

Delia crossed her legs, propped her hands on her knee, and leaned forward. "Go on."

Paul gave a sheepish smile. "I should also mention, this was not my finest hour. So, don't hold it against me."

She patted his arm. "We all have our demons. Don't let that stop you."

"One night my junior year, we won some big basketball tournament, and someone's brother bought us a couple of six-packs." Paul reclined, draping his arm across the back of the bench. "Anyway, we found ourselves on a farm road somewhere with a stash of firecrackers."

"So far a great combination," Delia stated. "A sixteen-year-old kid, testosterone, explosives, and beer. What could go wrong?"

"Exactly," Paul said. "Someone—and to be fair, it could have been me—thought it would be a fantastic idea to hide in the ditch along the side of the road, light these firecrackers and throw them at oncoming traffic."

"Your father may have had a reason for his anger."

"Wait for it . . ." He raised a finger. "We made up this game to see who had the better aim. And please understand, I'm not proud of this. We lit the firecracker, threw it from the ditch, and came up with a scoring system. One point if we hit an oncoming vehicle. Two points if the firecracker made it through the car's window."

"And? Did you win?"

He sighed. "I'm not sure winning would be an accurate description," Paul said. "Only one vehicle came down that road that night. And yes, I did get a firecracker in the window of that car. A Tyler police car."

"Paul!" Delia gasped, pushing his arms. "What were you thinking? You could have killed someone!"

"I know. Completely stupid. Thank God we didn't."

"So, I can laugh now?"

"Absolutely. I'd prefer you found this amusing. This stupidity happened nineteen years ago. Please, have a laugh at my expense."

"Thank you." The words escaped right before Delia's lips began to quiver. Seconds later a full belly laugh followed. She wiped her eyes. "I'm trying to imagine you, at sixteen, and the expression on your face when you realized it was a police car. It must have been an 'oh shit!' moment."

Paul nodded. "Exactly. My buddies were smart enough to make a run for it. As for me . . ." He held out his wrists. "I was arrested."

"And this is what you and your father fought over?"

"No." He shook his head. "Dad decided I needed to learn a lesson. He let me spend the night in the Tyler jail instead of bailing me out right away. So, here I was, the school jock, who put in the winning basket in some tournament and completely full of myself. But at my house, I had the father who left me in jail. I thought I'd show him." Paul laughed. "As soon as he bailed me out in the morning and I got home, I packed a bag and took off. I walked around Tyler for half the day until I calmed down. I ended up at Walter's house."

He thought back to the rainy night he knocked on Costa's door with his backpack on his shoulder and a surly expression across his face. After a week of Costa's loving reproach, he returned home.

Delia placed her hand on Paul's arm. "As a parent, what would you have done to your son?"

Paul looked away, lost in the memory. "The same. Probably. My dad did the right thing. I learned my lesson. My ego needed to be knocked down a notch or five."

Delia slid her hand back onto her lap. "You were lucky to have someone like Walter in your life. I wish I had an adult to look out for me when I was a teen. Maybe I would have made other choices," she muttered.

"When my parents died, he was a Godsend." Paul shook his head. "I have no idea what I would have done without him during that horrible time. We talked twice a week when I went back to school. He even came to visit me. Walter gave me all sorts of advice. On grieving. About my career path. He's the one who wrote my recommendation for graduate school. And when I finished grad school, he's the one who took me in while I got settled into, well, Ballentine. I owe him so much."

"What about Alejandro? Who's he?"

"Alejandro?" Paul asked. He shrugged. "Oh, he's the priest at Saint Daniel's. He's a good friend of Walter's. They've known each other for years."

"So, three confirmed bachelors," Delia said.

Tell her! screamed Paul's cautionary voices.

"Yeah." He chuckled. "Something like that. Walter and Al are also terrible gossips, so I don't tell them about my personal life." He looked at Delia. "I think it's one of the big reasons I have been—what did you say?—'mysterious' about my life in Ballentine. My time off is the only privacy I have."

"I can certainly understand, Paul. But the offer is open. Maybe we can go hang out in Tyler sometime." She smiled and nudged his shoulder.

Images of Allison, her boys, Chuck, and Brittany flashed through his head. Bishop Vance's words came back to him. *"Tyler is still a small town in many ways . . ."*

Paul glanced at Delia and said, "Sure. We can work something out if you want."

***

Abigail's text came in over Delia's car's Bluetooth: "Frank's lost his mind. Get in here ASAP."

Delia slapped her hand against her head while pressing the accelerator. Her gamble to sneak out for the afternoon backfired. She calculated: forty miles to the Dragon. It might as well have been 400 miles.

With the three new girls Frank hired for the Executive Concierge Desk, all of whom were eager to handle their share of the action, as well as Tawana and Abigail, Delia figured it would be a quiet Saturday night. Unless a few extra high rollers booked suites at the last minute, she wouldn't be needed for anything other than manning the desk for any last-minute theater ticket requests.

Her phone rang. "What's up?"

"Mr. Operations Manager is in a foul mood. Where are you?" Tawana asked.

Delia groaned. "I met Paul today. I should be there around six. I told Abs. She said she'd cover for me."

"She did. But room 1218 decided he wanted to upgrade his package. So, she's going to be busy for the rest of the night."

"Crap. I'm on my way. But I need to go home first because I'm not dressed for work."

Delia heard Tawana talking with someone in the background. She came back on the line. "Not a good idea. Abigail says Frank's heading to your house."

"I should have thought this through," Delia grumbled.

"Looks like your Texan is messing with your head," Tawana observed. "Delia, this is causing trouble for all of us. Not just with Frank, but now we're short-staffed. It's Saturday night."

"You weren't short-staffed when I checked the schedule this morning. The hotel was barely booked."

"Ah, so you didn't hear. Ito Yamano and his entourage came into town today. Last minute. He wants to inspect his oil fields before heading to the Mediterranean. I think he's planning on taking you on vacation with him."

Delia swore. "Any more bad news?"

"Not at this time. Hurry, okay?" Tawana said.

"I will. Tell you what. Leave your house key at the valet. I'll run to your place and grab something. Heaven only knows what will happen if I go home and Frank's waiting for me."

"You got it. I'm walking my key down now. But Delia, no more of this. Not on a Saturday. We're all losing money because of Mr. Texas."

An hour and a half later, Delia slipped behind the Dragon's Executive Concierge Desk. Tawana motioned toward the high roller hallway. "Mr. Ito is asking if you could join him for an in-room dinner and entertainment at your earliest convenience."

"I need a new job," Delia grumbled.

"Yes, you do." Tawana nodded. "Escort burnout is real. But lucky for you, my Oklahoman in room 1215 had a bit of a surprise. His wife showed up about thirty minutes ago. So, I'm off the hook and can cover the desk."

"Would you like to fill in for me with Ito?" Delia asked.

Tawana eyed her. "Damn, girl. Red's definitely your color. My dress looks better on you than me. Keep it, if for no other reason than for what you are going to have to endure when Frank gets ahold of you. I want the shoes back though. And no. Mr. Ito Yamano was very specific."

Delia rifled through the desk, grabbing condoms and throwing them in her purse. She snatched her security jewelry from the tray in the top drawer, slipping it on at record speed. Pushing out her chair she said, "Please tell him I'm on my way."

"Any reason *why* he had to wait for you?" Both women turned to see Frank standing behind them.

"Hello Frank," Delia purred, as she stepped aside.

He squeezed her forearm. "How about if I escort you so you don't get lost?"

She smoothed her hair with her free hand, pretending Frank's grip didn't hurt. "I think I can find the way," she said, her Southern drawl coming through.

Tawana shook her head and shot her friend a knowing glance.

"Let's go," Frank said, his teeth clenched. He didn't wait for her to establish her balance. Instead, he strode toward the high roller hall, half-dragging Delia with him. "I don't know what the hell you are up to," he hissed, tightening his grip. "But it stops. Got it? When you are done with Ito Yamano you come see me. If you don't, so help me God, I will make your life a living hell. Got it?"

"I got it," Delia said in a quivering whisper. In a louder voice, she exclaimed, "Let go, Frank. The high rollers don't like bruising."

Frank whipped his hand away. Delia lost her balance, took a step, and fell to the ground. "Get up!" he barked. "You been drinking? Or are you just stupid?" As she scrambled to her feet, he leaned in, his voice menacing as he said, "I expect to see you immediately when you are through. Then we'll settle this."

Chapter Thirteen

The Misunderstanding

Tuesday morning in late July, Paul left the rectory long before sunrise, too excited to sleep. For several weeks, there'd been schedule conflicts and work commitments on Delia's part, with her apologizing for being unavailable. On more than one occasion, she'd left town at a moment's notice, sending a text, saying she'd reach out when she could.

Delia said this happened every summer. As part of her duties with the Executive Concierge Desk, the operations manager sent her on last-minute public relations tours with little time to prepare. Impressed with her job responsibilities, Paul complimented her on having such a high honor. However, she showed little enthusiasm for her trips, making him secretly wonder if maybe she looked forward to their time together as much as he did.

With his free time, Paul painted Chuck and Brittany's nursery and built a crib for the baby. The bittersweet action temporarily eased the pain and regret he felt at not being able to have done it for his own son. However, that familiar longing was amplified when Chuck announced they were having a boy, and with Paul's permission, they wanted to name him Robert Patrick—their father's name.

As a distraction from missing Delia, as well as additional penance for the numerous infractions he knew he'd committed since he'd met her, Paul immersed himself in his church duties. Hoping to win a few points with the monsignor, he carried around the latest pop-Catholic philosophical reading material and commented on a passage here or there in conversation. For Costa's part, he only noted once or twice a week how his junior associate pastor spent more time closer to home.

Additionally, Paul brought up future projects for Saint Daniel's in conversation when the opportunity arose. Would the Ladies Auxiliary be willing to host a clothing drive for the Tyler Women's Clinic? Did the Knights of Columbus need assistance planning the Fall Festival? Would the local mission be sending their residents to this month's fish fry and if so, should Paul ask if Warden Shackleford would allow some minimum security prisoners to help out?

Paul invested considerable amounts of energy into the health and well-being of his parish. His focus kept him grounded enough to keep impropriety at bay, giving him hope his physical infatuation was subsiding and the next time Paul saw Delia, he would have more command of his thoughts. However, he knew the efforts he put into his duties constituted symbolic instead of substantive gestures. This worked well during the day, talking with Monsignor Costa, Father Morales, and Annie, all of whom commented on his on-fire approach to his ministry. At night, as he lay in bed, the truth danced around him: nothing about his vocation brought him joy. Worse, every Thursday visit for his prison ministry came with a thick dread and flashbacks of Armetta's lifeless eyes.

Now as the sun glowed in the distance, he hoped he hadn't overstepped by arriving before seven. Delia's text said to come, no matter how early.

Coffee in tow, he knocked on her door. When she didn't answer, he rang the bell. After five minutes, Paul pounded on her townhome's front door.

"What the fuck do you want!" Delia cried, wild-eyed when she opened up. Wearing a satin pink bathrobe, she paused from her fury and cupped her hands to her mouth. "Oh, Paul! I didn't . . . Oh . . . I'm so glad to see you!"

She laughed, embracing him while he balanced the coffees. Bringing her face forward, Delia planted a quick kiss on his mouth. Paul gulped, as if by doing so he would keep inside the pious thoughts he'd cultivated over the past few weeks.

"Come in!" She grabbed the coffee. "I'm so happy to see you. And look at you, Mr. Wainwright. You brought caffeine." She leaned into him, giving Paul a one-armed hug. Feeling slightly disoriented, he slipped his arm around her waist, resting his hand at the top of her hip. Putting her head on his shoulder, she said, "I've missed you."

"I've missed you, too," Paul laughed, drawing her closer. He cupped her chin, rubbing his index finger across the bottom of her cheek. "You have a bruise. What happened?"

Delia's fingers fluttered to her face. "Oh, that. Nothing." She pulled away. "I had a little run-in at the airport. Coming back from Europe. I ran into . . . the Customs sign." She glanced in the hall mirror, patting her hair. "Look at me. No, wait. Don't. Oh goodness! My hair looks like it has a mind of its own! Let me go upstairs. I'll be back in a few. Make yourself at home. Okay?"

Paul plopped onto the couch and turned on the television, an indulgence he saved for his downtime with Delia or basketball games with his brother. He listened to the upstairs shower and the Shreveport morning news combining into household music. These were simple noises representing a different life, which felt more complete than what he'd left in Ballentine less than two hours earlier. He'd dreamed of this life before seminary—a home, a woman who cared for him and who wanted to raise little ones who'd call him "Daddy." Closing his eyes, Paul became lost in the fantasy he'd forfeited.

The sensation of Delia's fingers ruffling his hair woke him. He lay a heartbeat longer, inhaling her vanilla perfume and transfixed by her touch. "Morning, Sunshine," she drawled, handing him his glasses. "You were wearing these when you fell asleep. I didn't want you to break them."

"Thanks." He sat, yawning. "What time is it?"

"Oh, a little after nine." Delia handed Paul his coffee. "I heated it up for you."

"Your bruise? I don't see it at all now."

"The makeup hides it."

"Please don't feel like you need to wear that gunk. You are just as pretty without all that stuff on your face."

"Well, thank you, Mr. Wainwright." Delia lowered her gaze while batting her eyelashes. "I'd rather wear it today. I don't want a lot of attention. That's all."

***

They sat in the gazebo at the Cushman Botanical Gardens, along the Red River later in the day. The summer afternoon cut off all expectations of a breeze. "Whew, it's hot," Delia said, fanning her legs with her skirt. She pushed Paul's arm. "I saw you, Mr. Wainwright. Don't think I didn't."

Paul smirked, slinging his arm behind her back, and resting it at the base of her hip.

The two spent the day strolling around the grounds, talking about their adventures in the past several weeks. Delia leaned against him, as she looked at his pictures of the crib he'd made for baby Robert. He talked in generic terms about his prison ministry and his time at Saint Daniel's, hoping his explanation suggested he volunteered at the church. If not, he theorized, perhaps it would be the opening he needed if she asked, to explain his role at Saint Daniel's.

She didn't ask.

He listened as Delia shared about her work and the numerous conventions at the Dragon. There'd been real estate groups, politicians, oil companies, and even the Order of the Moose held their international summit there two weeks earlier.

She rolled her eyes, groaning. "The Order of the Moose were an unusual group. Dirty old men with strange requests. Peanut butter pie and queso with saltines delivered to their room, NASCAR tickets. Their wives were even more demanding." She shook her head. "You and your prison counselors would be a dream."

"We'd want to use the pool and be left alone," Paul replied. "Prisoners can be a rowdy bunch. We'd be there for the quiet."

"I'll bet." Delia bit her lip. "I brought you something. And I want to tell you about it," she said. Fishing in her purse, she pulled out a burgundy velvet bag. "I bought this for you at the Vatican while I was in Rome a couple of weeks ago."

Paul reached in, pulling out a wooden crucifix. He gasped, "This . . . The intricacy! It's beautiful. Thank you, Delia."

"Handmade." She nudged her shoulder into his arm. "I met the man who carved it. He let me pick out the wood. I bought two. Yours is made from cedar. Mine's from cherry, hanging in my house already." She rested her hand in Paul's as her voice softened. "I spent plenty of time thinking these last few weeks. Gotta tell you. I've never met anyone like you."

"How do you figure?"

Delia shifted. "You. You're perfect, you know that?"

Paul opened his hand, interlacing their fingers. He offered her a lazy smile. "Hardly, but thank you."

"I've . . . well, I've done a lot of things in my life I'm not proud of." Delia paused. "I can see how I've made horrible choices. I met you and my life is starting to turn around. I have a ways to go, hard decisions I need to make. But I guarantee, these past few months have been almost miraculous. God sent you to save me." She tugged at his arm. "Don't laugh. I mean it. I have a confession. I hadn't told you because I didn't want you to think I was doing this for you. I began going to Mass."

"Wonderful!" he beamed, squeezing her hand.

She shook her head. "I am far from a state of grace. I'll get to confession at some point and then I'll take Communion. When I'm ready. When I've cleaned up everything. The power of spending time every Sunday with God renews me. And you!" Delia gently elbowed him. "You've got me praying before my meals. There've been complaints at the casino about me because I prayed before I ate. I was sitting with one of my clients and I asked for a quick moment to pray. I was written up for it, but I didn't care. God first."

"Delia, that's terrific. I'm so happy to hear about this," Paul said, rubbing her thumb.

She leaned in. "I find myself changing. Growing. Going to church has been a tremendous help. Sometimes I go in the middle of the week and sit there, just to have a quiet time with Him. You should see the church, Paul. Gorgeous stained glass. Carved pews. And the priest, Father LeBlanc! He's amazing. Next time you can stay over until Tuesday morning, I'll take you to All Saints. You'll love it."

"Sounds great," Paul's voice rose a half-octave as he began coughing.

"Here," Delia said, handing him her water bottle.

Paul released his hand from Delia's, took a drink, and then picked up her fingers, meshing them again with his.

Delia glanced at Paul. "I didn't change because of you. But I've changed because your example has inspired me. I'd never change for someone I date. You know that, right?"

"Right," Paul automatically stated, as he played through a simple question in his head: *Are we dating?*

***

"I wish you didn't have to go," Delia said at the end of the evening as they walked to her front door.

Pulling her closer, Paul glided his hand to the small of her back, leading her along the walkway. Her senses came to life with the intimacy of his touch.

"Me too . . . Early day tomorrow."

During dinner, Delia observed Paul continued to be physically attentive, yet he seemed lost in thought. Did he consider her admission about seeking God and going to church to be moving too fast?

And how did Paul define "too fast?" It took four months for him to give her a chaste kiss a few hours earlier. Since then, his emotional floodgates spilled open. All day, he'd connected to her, grabbing her hand, caressing her, and even—to Delia's complete astonishment—slipping his arm across her back and shoulders. His sensual touch suggested a propriety she found addicting.

"Is everything okay?" Delia asked. "Since dinner, I mean . . . well, you've been kinda quiet."

Paul eyed her, a wistful expression crossed his face. He reached over with his free hand, stroking her arm. "Have I? I'm sorry. I didn't mean to be." Shrugging, he said, "I got to thinking, I guess."

"Thinking about anything in particular?"

He ran his fingers across her arm, waking Delia's flesh. "Nothing really. Just our day together. You. Me. That kind of thing." His fingers brushed her cheek. "Your bruise. The makeup is coming off. You must have hit that sign hard," Paul said, as he planted a soft kiss on her cheek.

A jolt of energy shot through her face.

Paul's hands slid to Delia's waist. His fingers pressed against her hips, drawing her in. She gasped at the surprising sensation coming from the electric charge between them. Her pulse surged as he guided her closer.

Leaning forward, he kissed her forehead. "You have such a beautiful soul, Delia." Paul placed a kiss on her nose. "You are an extraordinary woman." He cupped her chin, tracing her jawline with his thumb. "And," he added before his lips reached hers, "I'm so glad you are finding your way back to Christ."

Paul kissed her with the passion of a thirsty man who had hiked far too long in the desert and Delia was his oasis. As they broke apart, he rested his forehead on hers. It ended up being a quick break in the action before several more rounds followed. When he pulled away for the final time, Paul traced her neck and collarbone. Whispering, he said, "Let's not go weeks without seeing each other. Way too long."

"Absolutely," Delia gasped.

Chapter Fourteen

The Message from Above

Sunday afternoon, Paul slipped out of the rectory's kitchen door. He paced under a sycamore tree, waiting for Delia to answer. After her plaintive hello, his words rushed out. "Are you okay? I just got your text."

"I'll be fine. I'm sorry, Paul." Delia's voice came through as short bursts.

"It happened at work a few days ago. Nothing's broken." She made a strangled sound. "A guy I work with . . . Look, it's just embarrassing. I don't want you to see me like this. I'm hideous. Next week, okay? Not tomorrow."

"No. I don't want to wait until next week." Rage percolated as he thought about the hell Delia endured at the hands of her coworker. "I want to come. I want to take care of you."

"All I need is rest. That's all. I . . . I . . ." Delia burst into tears. "I'm so sorry, Paul," she sobbed. "I'm so sorry."

Paul leaned into the tree, bracing himself as he listened to Delia cry. He said, "Hey now. Look. I can be there in a few hours."

"You don't have to. I mean it. My face is messed up."

He let out a soft chuckle. "I'm not coming for your face."

Delia stifled a laugh. "Really, I'll be okay."

"I want to help."

She sniffed. "That's what you said when I met you. Remember?"

Paul smiled. "I meant it then and I mean it now." When she didn't respond, he asked, "Delia? You there?"

"I'm here. You'd . . . you'd want to come? You'd want to see me like this?"

"I want to come," Paul said, his voice strong. "Of course I want to see you."

"But I'm all messed up."

"I don't care. Honestly. You could be missing your nose. It wouldn't matter to me."

"Thank you, Paul," she whispered.

Rushing up the stairs, Paul ran into his room. He tossed his clothes into his duffle bag.

"Slipping out early this week, Father Wainwright?"

He turned to see Father Morales in the hallway. A knowing smile spread across the older priest's face.

"I have some urgent business. I'll be back in a few days." Paul threw socks into his bag. He zipped the duffle closed and hefted it off the bed. He said, "Father, if you wouldn't mind letting—"

Morales walked into Paul's bedroom without an invitation. He said, "You go. Take care of your urgent Shreveport business. But eventually you will need to address your business here," he said, extending his hand and tapping Paul's head. "It'll catch up with you. Get in touch with me if you'll be gone longer than Tuesday. Right now, I'll plan on conducting Wednesday morning's Mass. Let me know if you need me to step in for your shift at the hospital Wednesday afternoon. I'll cover for you this afternoon when Monsignor asks where you are." Morales eyed him and let out a long sigh. "But Paul, when you come back from your urgent business, I suggest you consider taking that time off Monsignor Costa has been inviting you to take."

"I don't gamble, Father."

"I know that's not why you go to Shreveport," Morales stated. "However, it's best if you let Monsignor keep thinking you do."

After Morales left, the words hung in the room, leaving a haze of guilt for Paul to muddle through as he finished packing. He ran his hand through his hair, as his conscience confirmed Morales's sentiment. His life had resorted to secrets and lies.

Though he hadn't been truthful with his fellow priests and housemates, the realization he'd continued his charade with Delia gnawed through him. Paul recalled the memory from days earlier when she'd credited him for being her inspiration to return to church. Here he was, duplicitous with his behavior, and yet, she'd opened herself up, not only to him, but to God.

A woman so pure, so genuine, so honest—the traits which attracted him to begin with. Paul was living that secret life he didn't think he had. "What am I doing?" Paul muttered, zipping his bag. "She deserves better."

***

The hour-and-a-half drive took fifty-five minutes Sunday night. Paul rapped on the townhouse door but didn't wait for a response. "Hi," he said, poking his head inside.

He sucked in air as he took in Delia in the dim light. She lay on the couch.

Letting the bouquet of sunflowers hang at his side, Paul knelt next to her, scanning the purple and red blotches on Delia's face and arms.

He hissed, "What did he do to you?"

"My boss. He got mad," Delia said. "I pressed charges," she whispered. "I'm not backing down on that."

Paul moved a stray strand of hair off her cheek. "Are you in pain?"

"No. This happened Wednesday night. I . . ." Delia looked away. "It's just . . . I didn't want you to see me like this. I'm so ugly."

"All I see is your beautiful soul."

She extended her hand and ran it down Paul's arm, interlocking their fingers. "I can't believe you came. I can't believe you are seeing me this way and you aren't repulsed."

The electricity running through him brought by Delia's touch extinguished the cautionary voices in Paul's head. "Of course I'm here. Where else would I be?" he whispered as he planted a kiss on her mouth.

***

Monday night, Paul sat next to a curled-up Delia, his bare feet propped on the ottoman. The night before, he snoozed sitting in the same position, while she rested her head on his lap. He'd slept poorly, using the quiet hours of the night, while listening to her gentle breathing, to pray for healing for Delia as well as for strength and guidance for himself.

When the movie ended, she rose, stretched, and collected the empty pizza box. "Let me do that," Paul said.

"Sweet of you. But no thank you," she drawled. "I may have red blotches, but I assure you, I feel better than I look. I need the exercise." Walking into the kitchen, Delia giggled, while tossing her hair over her shoulder. She shook her hips. "What are you looking at, Mr. Wainwright?"

"Actually, I have a legitimate observation," Paul said, enjoying his view. "This is the first time I've seen you in shorts. You've always been in a dress."

"Dresses are required for the Executive Concierge Desk. Besides, I've always enjoyed dressing like a lady."

"Can I ask what happened at work?"

She wrinkled her nose. "Well, most people don't get the Frank-enstein special. I'm the lucky one. Frank is the one I lived with. He's the operations manager of the Dragon. We've been over for a long time, but Frank still thinks he owns me." She sat down next to him, tucking her foot underneath her. "Do you remember how I told you last week I was written up for praying before a meal with a client?"

"Yes," Paul said, reaching for her hands. "I remember."

"Wednesday night, Frank demanded I come in early Sunday morning for my shift." Delia frowned. "He didn't need me. He had plenty of coverage. But Frank likes to play games, and one of his games is to run me ragged. He hasn't done this to the other girls. That's why I've been so busy."

She rolled her eyes. "I put my foot down and told Frank I was going to church Sunday. I'd be in afterward," Delia said. "He told me I needed to rethink my priorities." She swallowed. "*'My priorities.'* God is my priority." She glanced at Paul, who hadn't lifted his gaze from her. "And, honestly, he had a point. I did need to rethink my priorities." She shrugged. "So, I quit."

Delia bit her lip. Looking away, she whispered, "And then he got pissed. As if me going to church and working on being a better person somehow threatened him. That's when I knew I made the right choice."

Paul leaned forward, kissing her fingers. "Good for you. It makes what this guy did to you so much worse. God is always the right choice."

Delia nuzzled his hand against her cheek. "Thanks, I doubt I'd have figured it out if I hadn't met you."

"What do you think you're going to do now?"

She leaned back. "I have a bit of money saved, so I'm okay. My home and cars are paid off. I don't have any bills. I'll sell my Honda. I don't need two cars. It'll pay for Maddy's expenses for her next school year. Saint George's Books—the Catholic shop where I bought your rosary—they're hiring. The shop owner goes to All Saints. I talked to her this morning. She offered me a job. It'll get me by for now."

"Do you think you are safe from Frank?" Paul asked.

Delia raised her shoulders then lowered them again. "I got an order of protection Thursday. Standing up to Frank and telling the judge . . . It was the hardest part. I'd let him push me around for so long," she said. "I've gotten those before, but this time it's different. I swear. I know it's going to sound crazy, getting *this* order of protection . . . It means I'll never go back to the Dragon. I'll never go back to all his games."

She ran her fingers through Paul's hair. "I'm done with the Dragon. And I meant it when I said Frank and I have been over for a long time. But before you, I didn't know what it was like to be treated right. To be with a real man," she said. "Thank you, Paul. You saved me."

Tell her! escaped one last screeching voice before Paul leaned in, becoming transfixed by Delia's kiss. He shut out all thought, reason, and logic, opting to experience the moment. Surrendering to his emotions, he let the last several years of loneliness wash away while the emotional overflow of her attention reinforced his soul.

As their kiss deepened, Paul slid his hand behind her neck, moving her hair aside. After breaking away, he moved his mouth to her shoulder, bathing her with tiny kisses. A small gasp escaped her lips, encouraging him to continue. He glided his fingers along the length of her side. Reaching the bottom of her shirt, he slipped his hand underneath and continued exploring. Delia moaned, reacting to his touch, as she fumbled with the buttons on his shirt.

"We could go upstairs," she suggested.

"I'd like that," he said.

Delia grabbed his hand, leading him to the staircase. Paul reached from behind, pulling her toward him. He whispered as his hands moved around her body. "I could carry you up the stairs. Like a grand gesture."

"Mmmm . . . You are doing plenty of other grand gestures, Mr. Wainwright," Delia said. "At this rate, we'll never make it to the bed. But then again—oh my!" she gasped.

All previous insecurities about what kind of performance he might have after being out of practice for so long flew from Paul's mind the more Delia's reaction affirmed his ego. As he heard her sweet sounds while exploring her body, climbing stair by stair toward her room, Paul knew he wouldn't last long once they hit the bedroom. With two steps left, he hungrily grabbed her waist, hoping to draw out their foreplay.

Delia leaned into him while gripping the banister. "You are making it very difficult to walk," she moaned, arching her back.

"I guess I'm doing this right."

Her legs trembled. She gasped again while bracing herself against the wall, letting Paul continue.

"Oh, yes . . . yes you are."

"Glad to hear it."

"Oh my . . . Mr. Wainwright . . ." She giggled. Her voice changed. "Wait! Are you okay?"

Paul released Delia, rubbing his head. "I'm fine. What was that?" he asked, looking at the piece of wood that had landed on him moments earlier when she bumped against the wall.

Bending, she picked up the object, holding it for his inspection. "It's the carving I bought in Rome. Your crucifix's twin."

Taking it from Delia, Paul examined the cross, turning the smooth wood in his fingers. Reality seeped back into his body. He sighed, "Well . . . rats."

***

Paul sat in Delia's wingback chair. He stared across the room, unable to face Delia.

"It's okay if you aren't ready," she said, now dressed and perched on the couch. Reaching over, she placed her hand on his leg. "Paul, I'm in no rush. Honestly."

"I need you not to touch me." Even to Paul's ears, his voice sounded robotic.

Delia yanked her hand away. "Did I do something?"

"No . . . give me a second, okay?" He put his head in his hands, letting his fingers spread his hair. It didn't feel as satisfying as when Delia had done the same moments earlier.

"Would you at least look at me?" she asked. "Please?"

He looked up, catching her eye. "I'm sorry. I've been supremely selfish. This." He pointed between them. "All my fault." The last sentence came out as a whisper.

"Paul—"

He raised his palm, signaling her to stop. "Let me finish." Without pretense he began, "I'm the junior associate pastor at Saint Daniel's Catholic Church in Ballentine. I'm an ordained Catholic priest. A *practicing* priest." Paul sighed. "Well, practicing in the sense that I conduct Mass and have other clergy duties. And yes, I also do conduct a prison ministry at the Ballentine Correctional Facility. I started it as a tribute to the memory of my parents."

He paused, waiting for her to react. When she didn't, he added, "Delia. I should have told you. I can't think of one acceptable excuse right now as to why I carried this on."

She glared, her jaw tight. "I see. You can't, huh?" He watched as her lip curled. "Well then, here's an idea, start with the unacceptable excuses."

Paul flinched. "I didn't want to admit to myself how I felt about you. I thought we could be platonic friends. That would be enough. It sounds foolish now." He shook his head. "I never could find a good time to tell you."

Delia threw up her hands. "Really Paul?" The agitation in her voice elevated. "How about when we first met on the side of the road? You might have mentioned it then. Or at lunch the following week? Those seem like they might have been ideal times to tell me." Standing, she wiped her hair back from her face with strong deliberate movements. Delia jammed her hands to her hips. "It never occurred to you there might be two of us invested in this relationship?"

"I truly am sorry. I should never have let this get out of hand. I hope you'll forgive me. I should have told you right away."

Delia stormed past him, her shoulders square. She flung open the front door. A look of contempt flew across her face, causing him to involuntarily clutch the sides of his chair.

Paul hung his head. "I didn't expect that I'd—"

She pointed toward the outside. "Get out!"

Chapter Fifteen

The Intervention

Tuesday morning, Paul shuffled downstairs, making a beeline to the coffee pot. "Welcome back," Morales said. "I trust your urgent business in Shreveport has been resolved?"

"I believe so," Paul grumbled, taking a seat.

Morales cleared his throat.

"Father Wainwright, I believe I overstepped Sunday afternoon. I'd like to ask you for forgiveness if I said anything out of line."

Paul concentrated on a robin sitting outside the rectory kitchen window. "Not at all. Your wise words are always appreciated." He picked up his coffee cup. "I'm probably due for a vacation."

"Probably."

He felt Morales's gaze. Paul asked, "On Sunday, why did you think I needed to fix my head when I came back from Shreveport?"

"Was I wrong?" Morales gave a short laugh. "It doesn't matter why. 'Shreveport' is another word for temptation. Every priest has been to 'Shreveport.' Given how late you came back last night, or should I say how early this morning, I'm guessing your business took care of itself."

"Yeah." He sighed, watching the robin fly away. "Pretty much."

"You look like death warmed over."

Paul raised his coffee cup, offering a toast. "Salud."

"Salud," Morales replied taking a sip from his cup. He gave a knowing nod. "If you need a confessor, of course, I'm here for you. If you'd rather have one who's mostly deaf, may I suggest Father Balzak at Holy Trinity in Longview? He's older than Monsignor and wouldn't recognize your voice." He drained his cup, stood, and patted Paul's shoulder as he walked toward the sink. "Let me know if you will be in a state of grace before tomorrow's Mass. Otherwise, I'd be happy to conduct it."

***

"Thanks for coming." Paul heard Allison say from the living room as he lay in Garret's bottom bunk. "All he's done for the past four days is sleep. Glad the boys are at their father's this week. They don't need to see their uncle like this. Chuck, I don't know what to do."

Paul stretched, pondering how much more penance he'd perform before discovering who would forgive him first: God or Delia. He checked his phone—noon. Allison hadn't asked questions when he arrived Tuesday evening, duffle bag in hand. Instead, she'd left him to himself all week. He saw now she'd lulled him into a false sense of security. Her ruse seemed to include Chuck. Penance would be a welcome reprieve from facing Allison.

As his siblings' voices grew louder, Paul knew he had borrowed time before one of them banged on the bedroom door. Picking up his rosary, he began his morning prayers. Hopefully, a more Divine presence might be on his side when he faced his sister and brother.

"You look like a melted cow turd in the July heat," Chuck drawled.

"Christ's Peace be with you," Paul grumbled. Drawing back his shoulders, he placed his left hand to his chest, parallel to the ground. Then, raising his right hand, and using the power of his priest ordainment, he offered his brother a blessing.

Chuck flipped him off.

"Boys!" Allison snapped, slugging their arms. "Chuck, take the plates and napkins. Paulie, you get the chips. I got the bread and sandwich fixings."

Sitting in the dining room, Paul reached across the table and opened the bread bag. He tossed two slices on his plate. As he grabbed turkey from the deli container, he saw his brother and sister staring, their plates empty. Chuck cleared his throat.

"Oh. Right." Paul flopped the meat onto the bread. Making the sign of the cross, he recited, "Bless us, O Lord, and these Thy gifts, which we are about to receive from Thy bounty, through Christ our Lord. Amen."

Chuck and Allison shared a glance. "So, Paulie," Chuck began. "What's new?"

Paul made a point of taking a long drink from his beer and then thoroughly chewed a bite of his sandwich. He washed it down with another swig, finishing the bottle, letting out an, "Ah . . ." Refusing to catch their questioning eyes, he rose, walked into the kitchen, returning with a fresh longneck.

"Why do you ask?"

Allison took charge. "You've seemed to have run away from Saint Daniel's for starters."

"Monsignor thought I needed a vacation."

"Okay," Allison said, drawing out the word into multiple syllables. "Why is that?"

"I appear to have a case of priest burnout."

"Well, you do seem pretty fucked up," Chuck observed.

Paul let out a scoff. "I'm fine. Or, I will be." He shrugged. "I was stupid."

Allison put her hand on her twin's arm. "Paulie, what happened?"

"I discovered last week I was dating a woman."

Chuck muttered, "I can't believe you were right." He whipped out his wallet. Looking at his bills he said, "I've got thirty."

Allison snatched the money from Chuck's hand. "You owe me twenty. And you are paying up."

"Ally thought you had a girlfriend," Chuck stated.

Paul grabbed the cash from Allison, placing it on the table. "I don't."

"But you just said—"

"I did have one." Paul let out a long sigh. "Apparently." He finished off his second beer. "I lied to her. To myself. Came clean Monday night."

"And?" Allison asked.

"It went as well as one can expect after seeing someone for four months."

"*Four months*!" Allison exclaimed. "Paul, you can't do that. You're a priest!"

"I'm aware," Paul said. He rolled his empty bottle between his fingers.

Chuck raised his eyebrows. "You know that's against the rules?"

"I believe Allison covered that," Paul said, his voice monotone as he studied the table.

"Obviously Paul didn't get the message," Ally said.

"Now hold on." Chuck lifted his hand to Allison. "Go easy on him. It's been a long time for our brother. Let's get all the facts first. Paulie, got a picture?"

Paul took out his phone, showing them the photo he'd snapped at the botanical garden. Delia wearing a green dress, with her hair cascading off her shoulders, sat on a bench, gazing at the pond next to her. The lump in his throat swelled as he pointed to the screen. "Delia."

Chuck blew out a low whistle. "Wow . . . She's hot. Way too pretty for the likes of you. But I'm impressed you've been two-timing God that long. Ouch, Ally." He rubbed his arm.

Allison grabbed the cash, shoving it in her pocket. "Four months counts."

"How'd you know about her?" Paul asked.

"I didn't. You've been acting weird. A permanent drippy grin plastered on your face . . . Running to Shreveport . . ."

At the mention of Shreveport, Paul winced.

"Four freak'n months." Chuck tilted his head. "She didn't figure out what you do?"

"I said I counseled at Ballentine Correctional," Paul replied. "True, but a lie by omission. There were several lies by omission, several half-truths." He hunched his shoulders, letting his head hang. "I don't know what I was thinking."

"I know what I'd have been thinking," Chuck commented, eyeing Delia's picture.

Allison said, "Paulie, talk to us. Delia is a symptom of a bigger issue."

Chuck sat back. "You know, I hate to say this because her ego doesn't need more help, but Allison's right."

"I'm not going to pretend I haven't thought about this. Well, to be fair, it's probably all I've thought about in the past few days." Paul frowned. "That and the prison riot . . ."

"What happened with the riot?" Allison asked.

"There were two captors, Foster and Armetta. Foster asked for me during the standoff. It was a weird request and the only one they had. So, the warden asked if I would come in, figuring if it was this simple, maybe they could end this without any bad publicity." Paul pinched the bridge of his nose. "By the time I'd gotten in there, Armetta had tortured the guards. One of them passed away in the past month from his injuries. Another is now blind and has a host of other issues. The last guy can't walk, which is also probably the least of his troubles."

"I remember hearing how those guards turned out," Chuck said.

"Foster wanted me to hear his confession prior to surrendering," Paul said, his voice low. "After we were done, he had me wait outside the storeroom where they were holed up. They got into a fight. When Foster let me back in, there was blood everywhere. Armetta's neck was broken. And his eyes . . ." He swallowed, hoping his voice stayed even. "They looked just like . . ." He waved his hand. "Never mind. You get the idea."

Chuck's fist hit the table. He turned away, swiping at his eyes.

Allison's hands flew to her mouth. "Just like Mom's and Dad's."

"Yep. Just like." Paul put his head in his hands, whispering, "I didn't see the fight. Foster is claiming self-defense. But there's more. It has to do with his confession, and it actually might be the worst part of this whole experience." His voice cracked. "I can't disclose that part."

"Fair enough." Chuck frowned. "That sucks, Paulie."

"Well shit," Allison spat. "To live through it again. Have you talked to anyone? At least about what you saw?"

Paul shook his head, "There's trauma and then there's 'let's dig up twenty-year-old Paul finding his dead parents who suffered a similar fate' trauma. I have to function. You know?"

Allison put her hand on Paul's shoulder. "No wonder the riot affected you."

"We understand," Chuck said.

"I know you do." Paul patted Ally's hand. "I was already second-guessing my vocational choices before the riot. Afterward, it's been worse. Then I met Delia. I fooled myself into thinking I could have a platonic relationship as if I didn't know what dating was. I just wanted a distraction from . . . from the riot." He snorted. "She was definitely a distraction." He pinched the bridge of his nose, shifting his head from side to side. "Like I told her, I didn't have any acceptable excuses for leading her on."

"Well, you do," Allison countered. Paul laughed. "No really, Paulie. You should never have entered the priesthood."

"Disagree," Paul said. "I was called."

Chuck coughed, "If you say so."

Paul watched Allison throw Chuck a warning side-glance before she said, "I know we've been through this, but hear me out. You say you had the calling. But I say you were really running away. You used grad school and then used the seminary as an excuse to avoid your grief."

"I'm sure I know—"

"You got home to find Mom and Dad's bodies. And a week later Kayla tells you what she did. You had a double whammy."

"'Double whammy'? A counseling term?" Chuck asked.

"Yes," Paul and Allison replied in unison.

Allison continued, "Chuck and I took time off when Mom and Dad died. We grieved. I didn't go back to Old Miss for a year. Chuck didn't even go back to college. We had each other. But you drove back to Tucson and started summer school a week after the funeral. The University of Arizona told you they'd hold your scholarship no matter what. But you still wanted to go to school, and you still played basketball. Paul, you even graduated the following summer. It was a lot in a year of tremendous loss."

"I wanted to move on," he mumbled.

"But did you?" Allison asked. "Or did you avoid moving on by jumping into grad school? Who gets a double master's in theology and clinical psychology? You told me at the time it was to help other men who lost their babies. I even remember talking to you and encouraging you to take a break. Next thing I know, you announced you felt 'empty' and were entering the seminary. Remember?"

"Yeah, I do."

"Paulie, you know that's not the way the whole priesthood calling works."

Chuck added, "I see where Allison's coming from." He glanced at his brother. "And I understand your position too. But gotta tell you, it's like you acted like you needed to continue punishing yourself for whatever part you think you played in those deaths—which, by the way, as we have told you before, you played zero part in those deaths. You know that, right?"

Paul ignored Chuck's question while he let his memories float back fifteen years earlier. Afraid to face his siblings, he said, "When Kayla told me she wanted to abort, I didn't come home until she promised me she wouldn't. I thought we were getting married. I dropped her off at her aunt's house. I thought I saved my son. If I'd stayed one day longer . . ." He looked at the two of them as he shook his head. "And then, because I stayed with Kayla one day longer meant I got back too late to save Mom and Dad. If I'd just managed to be here a day earlier . . ."

"Bro, no. You cannot blame yourself. There were three of them. They'd just been released and were going to do what they were going to do. If you'd been here, you don't know if it would have made a difference or if you'd be dead, too."

Allison added, "Oh Paul, to hold on to this guilt for so long . . ."

"That's not a calling, Paulie," Chuck said. "Seems to me you've been punishing yourself."

"You ever tell anyone about what Kayla did?" Chuck asked.

"No," Paul scoffed. "Only you two know. 'My former live-in girlfriend aborted our child' doesn't go over well in a Catholic seminary."

"Can appreciate that," Chuck conceded. "It would go over even worse now that you are a priest. Can you imagine? Even though you had nothing to do with Kayla's actions, it would be a huge scandal. Those in the congregation who are the most pious would probably be the ones least likely to forgive."

"Yeah . . . The outraged mobs forgetting about grace is not how I want to end my clergy career."

"It's not like the Protestants. Anyone can be a religious leader in those churches. The drug addicts and reformed brag how they found Jesus. They are welcomed by their church to share their journey to faith. But the Catholics!" Chuck sat back, turning up his palms. "Have any skeletons in your past, and the congregation will crucify you."

"Do you want to stay in the priesthood Paulie?" Allison asked.

Paul eyed Chuck and Allison. "It's the question I've been asking myself for a while. It isn't a simple one. I'd like to think, maybe there are more souls I can save. There're still parts of my job I find rewarding and some, not so much. Plus, I've made vows. However, there's a loophole. I can petition for a laicization if I choose to leave."

Chuck scoffed. "Leave it to the Catholic Church to have a long, pointless word to mean quit a job."

"Technically it means withdraw from the clergy. I'd need a good reason. Breaking my vows for Delia, or any woman, wouldn't be considered a good reason." Paul adjusted his glasses. "I can ask for laicization as long as I'm in a state of grace, which as of Tuesday afternoon's confession, I am."

Allison said, "I'd like to point out, you are only in a state of grace if you forgive yourself too."

Chapter Sixteen

The Choice

"I hate men," Delia groused, flopping into the booth Sunday afternoon. She batted a strand of errant hair away from her face. "And because of a *certain* man, I began going to church. And there are days, like today, when that is the last thing I want to do."

Tawana set her menu on the table and leaned forward. "Oh? This will be a good story." Propping her chin on her hands, she said, "Do tell."

"I went to church today because I do that now. I like it—usually—and I miss it when I don't go. Plus, I'm starting my new job this week. And it's a requirement to be a *practicing* Catholic to work at Saint George's Catholic Books and Gifts."

"Let's start again," Tawana replied. "Tell me about the first part, hating men. You've only been gone from the Dragon a week."

"Paul." She blew out her cheeks. "He's an asshole."

Tawana pursed her lips, while her continued blinking conveyed her surprise. "I thought last we'd talked, you and Mr. Texas had gotten together after Frank sent you all over the planet. You seemed so happy. Wasn't it when the two of you went to the botanical gardens? Didn't you tell me Paul finally gave you . . . What did you call it?" She raised her hand, rubbing her fingers, conjuring the words. "Oh yes, that 'Earth-shattering, toe-curling good night kiss'?"

"He was too good to be true."

"Oh no!" Tawana exclaimed. "Married, right?"

Delia slumped her head forward, letting her hands catch her forehead before her face hit the table. Composing herself, she caught Tawana's gaze. "He's a Catholic priest."

The middle of her friend's lips began quivering. The action spread, like a tidal wave, to the corners of her mouth. She swallowed before thunderous laughter bolted out of her. Tawana continued, clutching her side, as her volume increased. The sound rang through the restaurant, echoing off the floor, and landing in Delia's humiliated psyche.

"Get hold of yourself," Delia hissed, glancing around, afraid one of the restaurant's staring patrons might recognize her.

Propping a menu on the table, she hunched her shoulders shielding herself from prying eyes. When Tawana didn't show any signs of letting up, Delia pulled out her makeup mirror, checking out the remains of her facial bruises. Scowling, she applied foundation, while listening to her friend's hysterical laughter.

"Ha, ha, ha." She stuck out her tongue. "Are you done?"

"I think so. Sorry," Tawana said, taking measured breaths. She wiped her eyes. One last round of laughter escaped before she caught Delia's eye. "Oh, Sweetie, at least you found out before anything happened . . . Wait? That look on your face! You didn't!"

Delia clenched her teeth. "We were pretty darn close." She threw up her hands. "I can't believe he kept that from me!"

"Now just wait! Did you ever tell Mr. Texas Priest what you did for a living?"

"I quit my job before we went that far."

Tawana waggled her finger as her Southern drawl thickened. "No. No. No. Girlfriend. Don't give me that. You may be angry he lied to you, but how long were *you* misleading *him*? You were going to do the deed without letting him know your past? Which one of you is the bigger asshole?"

"It's my past. It's his present," Delia said, crossing her arms as she sunk into the booth. "He's the bigger asshole."

"Seems to me, your Texan should have a chance to weigh in on that."

***

After the first four days at Saint George's, Delia's inadequate Catholic knowledge, coupled with her lack of experience, festered, wearing down her self-confidence. Each customer interaction left her drained and feeling more inadequate than the last. Questions Ginny, Saint George's Catholic Books and Gifts owner, and Christina, the shop's other clerk, answered with professional ease, such as were the candles pre-blessed or where were the books on relics located, caused Delia to babble out the same response, "Let me ask."

The thought she'd been hired out of pity never left the back of her mind. Every night as she drove home, she wondered how long it would be before Ginny gave up on her, asking her to leave. And worse, making it so Delia would have to return to her job at the Dragon.

Friday morning, Ginny extended Delia a pleasant hello, tucked her arm through hers, and led her to the back room. "Welcome to the Order Desk," she stated, with more enthusiasm than the drab little room warranted. "Have a seat." She gestured toward the swivel chair next to the computer desk. "Online and phone orders come in here. We provide bulk supplies to

Louisiana, East Texas, Mississippi, and Oklahoma. When churches need anything, they send us emails or order online. Sometimes they will call. You also may get custom orders as well."

"Custom orders?" Delia asked, afraid she sounded foolish.

"For instance, someone who wants to emboss a name on a Bible. I'll sit with you today and we'll do this together." She gave her shoulder a pat. "Don't worry."

Delia cringed. She'd used similar words with new Dragon trainees who exhibited trouble grasping the finer points of the behind-the-desk aspects of the job. At the Executive Concierge Desk, acquiring theater tickets consisted of a simple phone call or a couple of clicks in the Dragon's entertainment software, which reserved the seats for the show and billed the hotel guest. Other services were handled through a software package and Frank's department. All she needed—while sitting at the desk at least—was a smile and to know how to use the computer's mouse. But at Saint George's, nothing proved to be as simple.

By late morning, when she hadn't made any significant mistakes, Ginny left her alone. Delia sat at the desk, searching through Saint George's catalog, hoping to familiarize herself with the product list.

Delia jumped when the phone rang, taking away her concentration. "I'm looking for missals," a man said with a Caribbean accent after she answered. The inflection of his voice put Delia at ease, as if she'd heard it before.

"I beg your pardon?"

The man replied, "Missals. I need to order two hundred of them."

A glimmer of recognition registered. The voice sounded like Anton, one of the Dragon's bartenders, who always came by to say hello to the girls on the twelfth floor on Friday afternoon. For years, Anton and a few other longtime Dragon employees threw an impromptu happy hour before their Friday afternoon shift, complete with cocktails and an occasional recreational drug.

At the thought of Anton and Friday afternoons at the Dragon, wistfulness crept in. Delia missed her friends. Homesick and wanting to hear the man's voice again, she licked her lips then asked, "Please tell me more about these 'missiles'?"

"I need Spanish missals in particular," the caller said.

Delia burst out laughing as a familiar warmth washed over her. It would be like Anton to call Saint George's to say hello. She crossed her legs, leaning into the desk. "We don't have missiles, rocket launchers, or flamethrowers either. Anton, it's good to hear your voice, though," Delia drawled, adding a flirty laugh. "Tell you what, Babycakes, how about I come by and see you this weekend?" For the first time since starting her job, her confidence bloomed. "Is Tawana with you? Abigail?"

"I'm sorry? This is a *Catholic* store, right?" the man asked.

She felt a grip on her shoulder. Stiffening and afraid to move her head, Delia's neck flushed. Ginny said, "We carry missals. Those are the books found in the pews of every Catholic Church, everywhere. The ones with the prayers, readings, and songs for each week."

Delia opened her mouth, closed it, and opened it again.

"Hello?" came the voice from the other side of the line.

"Hand me the receiver," Ginny said, without masking her waning patience. "I'll take it from here."

That night, as she walked into her townhome, Delia dropped her keys on her kitchen counter. She placed her take-out dinner and dessert from Verona Italian next to them and kicked off her shoes. A wave of depression crashed over her. Friday nights were meant for fun and friends—this Friday especially. Thinking back, she didn't remember a time she'd spent a Friday night alone. High school? Maybe? But probably not even then.

Delia didn't bother with her main course. Instead, she opened the smaller Styrofoam container, inhaling the chocolate ganache aroma. As she unwrapped her plastic fork, she managed a quick scan of the room for a candle, almost relieved she didn't have one on hand. What was more pathetic, she wondered: lighting a candle or singing *Happy Birthday* to herself?

Stabbing a bite of her cake, she ate, fighting the loneliness. Delia pondered how today might have been different if Paul were still in her life. If he hadn't lied to her. Would they have spent the day together? The futile exercise brought out other thoughts. For him to have spent her thirtieth birthday with her, he'd have lied to the other people in his life—potential victims of Paul's deception.

She shoved her fork into the cake again, bringing another bite to her mouth. Would this be her life after the Dragon? Weekends alone eating take-out after a week of faux pas after faux pas at Saint George's? How long would Ginny tolerate such nonsense? For as much as she talked about leaving the Dragon behind, Delia doubted she had an aptitude for anything else.

The desperation to reach out to Abigail and Tawana consumed her. She shook it off, recognizing they were working. Right now, she knew they were eating something more interesting than take-out. They were enjoying their evening, not sitting at home listening to the quiet. And most depressing of all, her friends were in the arms of Dragon clients who were just as lonely as Delia.

Her phone buzzed. Delia glanced at the message from Maddy. Tommy texted earlier in the day. Mama's call came in around ten that morning.

She listened to her voicemail when she stepped out for lunch. After the humiliating misunderstanding with the *Roman Missalettes*, she had decided not to call her mother back right then, afraid she'd end up admitting how her week had shaped into a hodgepodge of incompetent disasters.

Another text message came in. "Happy birthday, Gorgeous. I miss you." Delia floated her hand above Frank's text, itching to reply. Before she finished considering her answer, he sent another note. "We're short-staffed. Wanna make a few bucks using your best talents? It's your birthday, so I'll give you the entire cut if you'll help me out."

Delia let her hand hover over the phone a moment longer. Listening to the sounds of her home's silence radiating around her, she wondered how she would adjust to such a boring life. Wasn't this what she wanted? To move on from the Dragon? Or was leaving the Dragon only her goal when she thought Paul held promise for a future?

"The devil you know or the angel you don't." She strummed her fingers on the counter, relieved to hear noises.

To her surprise, Frank didn't text again. In their long relationship, he never took the multiple orders of protection Delia sought with any serious consideration. However, an inkling in the back of her mind made her think that by not receiving a reply to his text, he now believed this might be the time she turned him in.

Sitting straighter, she deleted his message. "One more text from you, asshole, and I call the court," Delia muttered while she resolved not to ruin the remainder of her day with any more thoughts of Frank. Picking up her cell again, she scrolled through her contacts.

"Hi Mama," Delia said. "How about I take you to lunch tomorrow? We can swing by and pick up Maddy on the way."

Chapter Seventeen

Sins of the Father

Paul shifted, looking for a comfortable position in the wooden seat. With little area in front of him, he crossed his legs, first at the ankles, then at the knees, and finally settling with his left calf over his right thigh. None of the positions gave him more space. Next to him sat Monsignor Costa, cramming Paul into the corner between the wall and the desk, oblivious to his discomfort.

Deciding his lack of sufficient room constituted a chance to grow through personal suffering, he let his restlessness go, knowing the Creator had greater issues to focus on. Instead, he glanced out the window at the grassy lawn in front of Saint Daniel's, grateful to be in a room with sunlight. Bishop Vance, who had commandeered Monsignor Costa's desk, sat across from him, sifting through papers, making "hmm . . ." and "interesting . . ." noises which Paul wished he could drown out more than he wished he could produce additional space for his legs.

The calendar on Costa's office wall read September, which meant another yearly evaluation. As part of this tedious process, Monsignor asked Paul to write his own assessment about his performance in the Saint Daniel's community during the last year.

The performance evaluation included metrics: the number of Masses, marriages, baptisms, and funerals Paul conducted. He listed the income for Saint Daniel's brought in as a direct result of his work. Additionally, he provided a list of other activities he participated in throughout the year, for the betterment of God, the parish, the salvation of souls, the community of Ballentine, as well as his own professional and spiritual growth. To quantify the unquantifiable, Paul added a narrative, discussing his day-to-day ministries around the community, his work visiting shut-ins through the Saint Vincent dePaul Society, the counseling of unwed mothers at the Tyler Women's Clinic, as well as an in-depth summary of his Thursday afternoons at the Ballentine Correctional Facility.

After seven years in the priesthood, the meeting didn't concern Paul. He knew what to expect. However, the entire act of dredging up memories of the past year, in order to make the report in the first place, gave him a week of acid reflux. Putting together a self-assessment brought back his doubts and transgressions, none of which made it into the review. Nowhere in his report did he have a line item for "going through the motions" because, if he were being honest, this year's evaluation felt more like embellishment and less like a true assessment of his duties.

"You're modest, Father," Vance said, scanning Paul's file. "As I recall, you helped settle that awful prison riot back in April. I don't see that in here."

"Overlooked, Sir," Paul said. "I think my role in that might have been exaggerated by the prison staff."

"Father Wainwright was exceptional. Saved those guards," Costa said with a pleased expression plastered on his face. He turned to Paul, patting his back. "Didn't I hear your prison ministry doubled after that incident?"

"One guard died. There'd been much interest afterward, yes," Paul said. "However, it seems to have waned as time has gone on. I'm not sure if it was just a curiosity of what happened or if . . ." He shrugged.

Bishop Vance scanned the pages a second time, making "uh-huh," and "oh yes, I remember," noises at random intervals. "I don't see anything about personal growth. I do require my priests to go on an annual retreat. We all need spiritual growth. We talked at your review last year about you not taking time off. Did you take a retreat this year?"

Paul coughed, as he thought about the week he'd slept on his nephew's bed. "I, uh . . . last month."

"Where'd you go?" Vance asked. "Personally, I'm a fan of Tepeyac Abbey outside of Mexico City. Ever been there? Such an amazing place!"

"Tepeyac . . . I'd like to go there sometime," Paul said.

Vance nodded. "Never met anyone who didn't come back refreshed."

Costa cleared his throat and motioned toward Paul. "I'd like to add, I also know Father Wainwright here spent his free time this summer ministering in Shreveport, helping at All Saints, as well as providing Communion to shut-ins over there, and working with their local Saint Vincent dePaul Society." Costa beamed. "I believe you conducted Mass there on a few occasions and held confessions for Father LeBlanc?"

"Uh . . . well, yes," Paul said, feeling the color drain from his face. "I was unaware you knew about all of those activities . . . other than the one occasion I helped with the funeral Mass."

The monsignor laughed. "Father LeBlanc and I go way back to seminary. We'll be traveling to Rome together in the spring. I thought you knew we were old friends."

"Maurice LeBlanc?" Vance asked. "Great priest. Inspiring."

"Small world," Paul muttered.

"Indeed," Costa agreed.

The bishop peered over his glasses. "Are you still finding occasion to go to Shreveport and help on your days off?"

Paul shook his head. "Recently I've been staying closer to home."

Vance placed the report on Costa's desk. He studied Paul. "Father Wainwright, when we talked in the summer, I asked if you were happy here. You assured me you were."

"And it's still the case," Paul said. "Monsignor and Father Morales have been exceptional role models and mentors."

"Of course," Bishop Vance agreed. "I want to address the elephant in the room. I have serious concerns about your prison ministry. There are already non-profits which do this kind of thing, trained for these kinds of situations." He eyed him long enough for Paul to shift in the chair and recross his legs. "There have been concerns . . . Our insurance may not cover you or any incident you are involved in. And, to be honest, I have concerns about *you* specifically and this ministry."

"I don't think you have to wor—"

Vance cut him off. "There is so much more you could be doing for this parish, for our diocese. I think it's time for you to direct your activities to other areas in the community."

"Such as?" Paul asked, his neck muscles tightening as he tried to keep his voice even.

Vance sighed. "Well, I'll give you some time to decide. Say, the next six months to wrap your ministry up? Of course, you are overdue for a transfer. I think there's going to be an opening in Texarkana or Lufkin next summer." He gestured to Costa. "The monsignor and I need to discuss this further. Perhaps we can have this conversation after he returns from Rome."

"I would rather not end the prison ministry," Paul said, now perching on the edge of the chair. He flexed his fingers and balled them into fists. "Is this because of my past and what happened with my parents? I've always thought if there was a way to save another soul and perhaps stop anyone else from experiencing what my family went through . . ." He paused, swallowed, and continued. "I feel called . . ."

"No doubt, you do feel called," Vance said. "However, there are other ways to use your talents."

"Have there been complaints about the ministry?" Paul asked, his voice rising.

"Not at all," Vance said. He turned to Costa. "Have you heard anything one way or another?"

Monsignor Costa leaned forward, a kind smile spread across his face. "Warden Shackleford has only been positive about your work there. Please understand, Father, after watching you all these years, and through prayer, I've come to the conclusion this just seems to drain you more than it brings you the kind of joy that comes from serving."

Bishop Vance added, "I've given this a great deal of prayer and thought. This will be an opportunity to strengthen your faith. I'm certain you can discern other areas which might be a good fit for you."

"Such as?" The blood pounded in Paul's temples. "I'm having a hard time understanding your point."

The two elder priests exchanged a look. "There are always ways to serve, Father. It just won't be at the prison," Monsignor said. "I'm sure you can find something that suits you. Just pray on your next steps. The path will be made clear."

***

"So, Father," Morales said over breakfast at the Wagon Wheel a few days later. "Any decisions?"

Paul swallowed a sip of coffee. "Not really." He turned his palms up. "I'd do more at the Tyler Women's Clinic if I could. But I had to make a pest of myself to help there in the first place. There's so much community outpouring of help with that one; babies and women in distress are much more exciting for volunteers. I'm blessed to have my twice-a-month counseling slots." Shrugging, he added, "The prison ministry. It is the only ministry that's truly mine. I can't think of anything I'd rather do."

Morales laughed. "Listen to you. Bishop Vance and the monsignor won't let you off the hook. You've been offered a blank canvas. What will you paint?"

"I like what I do there," Paul challenged. "I've reached some of the inmates. Hopefully I've helped them heal. For me, it's been rewarding."

"I think you are missing the bigger picture," Morales said.

"Which is?"

"There's more to you than the prison ministry. I know it. Monsignor knows it. And Bishop Vance certainly knows it. They think you are hiding behind it. It's a weak excuse for not truly exploring what else you could be doing."

He shook his head. "I don't see that to be the case."

Morales pointed a finger at Paul. "Exactly. You're busy hiding. The prison is hiding. And, dare I say, Shreveport was hiding."

There'd been no discussion between the two of them about anything to do with Paul's previous summer in Shreveport. Morales's comment made him more uncomfortable than he wanted to let on, wishing instead to put the entire incident behind him. Even Chuck and Allison seemed to steer clear of any mention of their brother's summer.

Morales continued, "The question is, what are you hiding from?"

Paul said, "I can't hide from God. So, I doubt I'm hiding from anything."

"Ha!" Morales scoffed. "If that's the case, don't make yourself miserable by hiding the truth from yourself," he said.

"I'm not following."

"There are stories. They reach all of us." Morales eyed Paul. "You're a good priest, Father. But let's face it, you are at Saint Daniel's because of Monsignor Costa." Morales sat back, studying Paul. "Alrighty then, judging from the expression on your face, perhaps you hadn't put it together. Monsignor asked for you specifically when you finished seminary. Why is he holding on to you? Is he sentimental? That's my guess. You are still that young man, the boy he's known his entire life, the one he wants to take care of. So, what do *you* need to do so he can let you go?"

***

The following Monday evening, with Father Morales's words ringing in his head, Paul drove into Tyler, wearing his favorite Mavericks t-shirt and a Rangers ball cap. Though he might pay for it later, he opted to leave his glasses in his truck. He walked into Saint Luke's Hospital, the same hospital where he was born and had visited as a member of the clergy. As he climbed the front steps, Paul asked God for the selfish request not to be recognized.

After Paul followed the signs down the hallway to the meeting room, he bypassed the coffee and stale store-bought shortbread cookies, only giving cursory nods at the other men, milling around the snacks. Spotting a seat in the back row on the aisle, he sat, stretching out his long legs. In hopes it would deter others from coming in his direction, he became immersed in the literature he'd been handed. As an added measure, Paul plopped his Ranger's hat in the seat next to him, suggesting he was saving it for another. While he waited, he closed his eyes, letting his prayers battle with his internal demons.

"Hello," came a voice. Paul opened his eyes to see a balding man. His eyes flickered with a fierceness, but the rest of his face gave off a look of compassion and vulnerability, which resonated with Paul. "For those of you who are new, welcome. I'm Mitchell Ryan." There were murmurs of hello from the crowd. "And you all know where you are, right?" He offered a small smile. "This is Stolen Voices. We are a grief support group for men who have lost a child through abortion."

With those words, several men in the room shuffled in their chairs, covertly eyeing the crowd, as if they wanted to make sure they weren't alone. Paul cast his gaze down, wishing he'd stayed at the rectory, unsure if coming had been a good idea. Slouching in his chair, he grabbed his hat, adjusting the brim low on his head.

Mitchell continued, "Thank you all for coming. If you want to share your story, we are here to listen. If you want to sit back and just observe, that's cool too. But just know, brother, you aren't doing this by yourself any longer."

When the meeting ended, Paul left drained, yet relieved. Throughout the night, he'd been torn between wanting to stay anonymous and wanting to turn to his priest role, offering comfort, counseling, and guidance to these devastated men. Even though he felt an immense reassurance knowing he wasn't alone on this journey, he said nothing during the meeting, choosing the role of a quiet spectator. However, he found himself astonished at how many of these men's personal stories of depression, guilt, and shame were similar to his own.

As he drove back to Ballentine, he thought, not for the first time, of what his child might have been doing at this stage of his life. Would he be a basketball player? Would he and Kayla have had four more? Would there have been any twins? The fantasy about how his son's life would have played out wasn't new, but the Stolen Voices meeting showed him how far he'd shoved his grief and trauma away.

With twelve miles to go, Paul turned off onto the quiet country Texas road leading to Ballentine. He thought of Costa and Morales in the rectory's living room playing cribbage or chess while debating theology, just as they did most every night. He dreaded knowing he'd have to walk past both priests when he returned, with them expecting Paul to engage in polite conversation. Paul flipped on his turn signal and pulled into an empty feed store parking lot. With shaking hands, he put the truck in park. By the time he managed to cut the engine, the shaking worked its way into his entire body. The grief he'd suppressed for years raced to the front of his thoughts, begging for the attention he'd long denied. Unable to control what he'd dammed inside, everything he'd been holding back came bursting through in a storm of emotions. For the first time, Paul Wainwright wept for the son he never held.

Chapter Eighteen

The Sign

"Sorry I'm late," Delia said, shrugging off her coat. She collapsed into the booth.

"How was your date?" Tawana asked.

Delia rolled her eyes. "Who are these men? Seriously T. It was so much easier at the Dragon. They didn't want to talk about science fiction movies for hours on end. *This* guy though? Don't get me wrong. He may have been sweet, but I knew he wasn't for me when he arrived at the restaurant wearing a 'Live Long and Prosper' t-shirt." She waved her hand, "He said it's a reference to a 1960s sci-fi show. I tuned him out ten minutes after we met."

"Mr. UFO wasn't a love connection?" The trace of a smile formed around Tawana's lips.

"He was better than the last guy," Delia grumbled.

"Well, let's face it. If anyone shows up on a first date with handmade cloth dolls and announces those dolls represent you and him, and then says, 'If we have a fight, our doll-likenesses can talk to each other and work it out,' there's a good chance the men you go out with afterward can only be better."

"You forgot how the dolls were supposed to act out sex on the restaurant table so he'd know what I liked," Delia laughed, wiping her eyes.

"Look on the bright side. At least he didn't recognize you from your last job."

She groaned. "There've been a couple of men who have. Totally humiliating. I want to put my past behind me." She looked around, making sure nobody noticed them. "T, what do I do? I'm trying to change my life. That isn't me anymore.

"I understand. You *are* changing, Delia."

"And then to find men on that dating app who recognized me!"

"I'm thinking you need to find a better dating app," Tawana said.

"Well, I think I'm done with meeting men online. I've got a date this weekend with Ken, the guy I met at the gym."

"The muscular blond who walked you to your car after our yoga class?"

"That's him. He seemed nice. We stood in the parking lot and talked for a while. If he doesn't work out, maybe I'll give up." Delia wrinkled her nose while tightening her jaw. "I hate to say this, but Paul treated me well. I actually wanted to have a second date with him. Too bad he turned out to be an incredible asshole and a pathological liar."

"Your description of Mr. Texan seems unfairly harsh," Tawana commented.

"No, it isn't," Delia claimed, as her chin rose upward. "Paul led me on for months. He even told me he lived with a woman. He said he had a child who died. There's no way that can be true. And you want to know why?" She flattened her hands on the table. "Because he's a priest. Priests don't live with women and have babies."

"Did he lie about other things?"

"How would I know?" She shrugged. "I mean, I've thought back over our time together. But it doesn't matter, does it? Even if he didn't lie about anything else, let's face it. The priest part is a bit of a deal breaker, don't you think?" Delia snickered, "Though, in the end, he kind of forgot about the whole celibacy thing."

"I'm not defending him, Sweetie, but is it possible he was telling the truth about the girlfriend and the kid?" Tawana asked. "That could have happened before he became a priest. Think about it. He was totally into you and didn't want the magic to end. Maybe what he said was true about his life, except for leaving out the priest part." She put out a hand, stopping Delia's next protest. "You were totally into him too. What part of *your* life weren't you truthful about?"

Delia folded her arms, leaning back in the booth. "It wasn't the same, and you know it."

"We will have to agree to disagree," Tawana drawled. "You sure are still hung up on him."

"Not true," she scoffed. "I'm just pissed. He lied to me."

The old conversation never brought Delia a satisfactory ending.

"You said he apologized," Tawana pointed out.

"What was I expected to say? 'It's totally okay. You're welcome to play with my heart any time'?"

"Seems a bit dramatic, but if it works for you."

Delia threw up her hands. "I just don't understand. What was Paul's end game?"

"What was the end game with the men at the Dragon?"

"Oh, come on! You and I both know there's nothing to that. We provided a service. A night of fun and a happy ending for them. No commitment. No strings. There's an understanding."

"And here you are, questioning Paul because he didn't treat you like a call girl."

Delia glared at her friend.

"What will it take to forgive him?" Tawana asked. "And more to the point, how is what he was doing less forgivable than what you were doing with Dragon clients? How do you think those wives and girlfriends feel? You know plenty of them figured out what was going on. Many were just in the next suite when their men were busy with you."

"It isn't the same."

"If you say so," Tawana replied. "But you know what I think? You wanted Mr. Preacher Man to save you from the Dragon. You didn't think you could leave on your own. You thought he was your white knight, prepared to whisk you away. And then you found out he wasn't perfect."

Delia studied her nails, refusing to catch her friend's eye. "I could use a manicure," she mumbled.

"Look, you can bury this under the couch all you want, but eventually you are going to have to move the furniture," Tawana said. "So, until you find a way to make peace with Mr. Preacher Man, you aren't going to be able to move on. What if the next guy who comes along isn't Frank, doesn't play with dolls, and treats you the way Paul did?"

Delia sighed, "I think I'd be in Heaven."

"At the rate you're going, it might take you that long to find someone," Tawana said.

"Are you done?"

"With your Texan? For now." Tawana straightened and cleared her throat. "I have news."

"Do tell," Delia said, relieved to be off the topic of Paul.

"I quit the Dragon."

"Yeah? When?"

"Two weeks ago. Decided enough was enough. You inspired me. I want a job with weekends off and less pay. I have an interview tomorrow with Louisiana State Bank. They're hiring tellers."

Delia laughed, "It'll be worth the trade-off. And you are right, much less pay. But I have to tell you, for the first time in my life, I'm proud to tell people what I do. Plus, my boss doesn't pound on my door at all hours demanding sex. So, that's a bonus."

***

Delia met Ken Saturday night at the Bayou Steakhouse. He greeted her with a bear hug at the entrance. With a possessive hand slung low on her back, he'd escorted her to their table. Ken motioned for the waiter, "Scotch rocks," his voice boomed. Leaning down, he licked his lips as he stroked her chin. "Whatever you want to drink, Baby. It's on me."

Ken insisted on ordering dinner as soon as the waiter brought the scotch and Delia's water. In the time it had taken for her to empty half her glass and eat a piece of bread, they'd covered the first date background basics. By her second slice, she'd wondered what had attracted her to Ken days earlier. The more he talked, the more he reminded her of the kind of Dragon guest who didn't measure up to a high roller's suite, and yet, thought he deserved all the perks anyway.

"So, what do you do? I never asked." Delia propped her chin on her hand.

Ken leaned back, sipping his scotch. He cocked his head. A lazy grin crossed his face. "I work for Luxe Cadillac off King's Highway. Top salesman last year."

"Oh? How interesting."

"Yeah, great job," Ken said, giving Delia the once-over. "You're too hot to be driving a Toyota. I could see you driving a Caddy. We can set you up on a seven-year lease. It lets everyone think you have money even when you don't. What are your payments on your car? I can do better."

Delia plucked her napkin from the table and unrolled the silverware. She smoothed the cloth over her skirt, making sure she attended to every wrinkle. "Thanks, but I bought my Camry a few months ago. I'm good."

"Fine for now. But I like my women to drive with style, so we aren't done with this conversation." He winked as he downed the last drops from his glass. "So, what do you do? Model? Hot librarian?"

Delia fiddled with her necklace while coming up with a respectable way to quell Ken's comment. "The librarian thing is somewhat close. I work with books in a way," she stated. "I work at Saint George's—"

"I knew it!" Ken roared, pumping his fist. "I can always guess these things." He pointed at Delia. "It's one of my many gifts."

Before she could process his comment, the waiter returned. Ken pointed to his empty glass. "I need another."

"Certainly," the waiter replied, setting their salads in front of them. He added, "Is there anything else I can bring you?"

"Yeah, I guess you didn't hear me," Ken sneered while waving his empty glass in the waiter's face. "Do I have to do your job for you? Another drink."

"Of course," the waiter said. He nodded to Delia, checking to ensure she found her food acceptable. She pursed her lips as she threw him an apologetic half smile.

Ken grumbled, picking up his fork, "Well, shit. Good service shouldn't be so difficult. What the fuck's his problem?"

"I'm certain he was only making sure we didn't need anything *other* than your drink," Delia said. "Excuse me, please," she added, bowing her head while making the sign of the cross.

"Wait!" Ken said in a hoarse whisper. He rapped his knuckles on the table next to her plate. "What are you doing?"

Delia glanced up in time to see Ken looking around the restaurant. "Are you praying? Now? Oh, Jesus. People can see us." He slumped in his chair, putting his hand in front of his face. His eyes shifted from side to side. "Well, shit! Are you one of those religious chicks?"

Reaching across the table, she patted Ken's arm. "Not to worry, I just need a moment. You're welcome to join me if you'd like."

"You could've told me," he grumbled.

Delia finished her prayer. She smiled as she picked up her fork. "Yes, I pray before I eat."

Ken crossed his arms. "That's cool. I guess," he said. "I didn't mean to treat you like a freak. If you hadn't surprised me . . . I take it with the weird hand thing you did, you're a Catholic?"

She gave a slight nod.

"So, if you're a Catholic, I guess you're a virgin." Ken looked conciliatory. "So, sex is out tonight?"

"Well," Delia said, "I don't sleep with men on the first date." *Anymore.*

"Oh, that's promising. I don't mind waiting until we go out again. What'cha doing tomorrow night?"

"Bible study."

Ken waggled his eyebrows. "Not to worry, I love a challenge."

***

"How was your date?" Christina asked the following Monday. Since Delia started at Saint George's, the two had become fast friends.

"I've decided it's time for me to stay away from men for a while."

"And why is that?"

"The date was horrible. I sent him a text this morning. I thanked him for dinner, wished him well, and stated the obvious: we have different goals—which was the kindest way of saying I thought he was an idiot." She shook her head. "I need to be single for a while and see where that leads me."

"Listen, have you talked to a counselor? I'm not trying to pry but you told me about Frank and that other guy . . ."

"Paul," she said through clenched teeth.

"Look, Delia. Women say things like they want to be single for a while when they haven't resolved their past relationships. You obviously have some pent-up anger," Christina said. Delia raised an eyebrow. "Don't stare at me like that. You've growled enough about your Paul guy. He was perfect until he found a way to break your heart." She wagged her index finger. "You aren't over him."

It took Delia a full minute to let her laughter completely fade. She wiped her eyes. "You sound like my friend Tawana. I assure you, there's nothing left to resolve. Paul's not coming back."

"It isn't what I meant," Christina replied. "I think you two have unfinished business. Something that still needs to be said."

"Paul said enough for the two of us," Delia grumbled.

"Your anger comes through in your voice."

Delia raised an eyebrow, "I'll eventually stop being angry."

"Who's your anger hurting?" Christina asked. "He may have moved on from you, but you are the one having a hard time moving on from him." She added, "I would hate to see you make a pattern of these kinds of men."

After lunch, Delia sat at her back-office desk, working on the day's online orders. A sudden commotion in the shop startled her.

"Delia! Get your sweet ass out here!" The aggressive male voice shouted from the front of the store. *Ken.*

She recognized the frenetic anger coming from his words—the same kind of tone Frank used when her life was about to become ugly. Though she wrapped her sweater tighter, an unmistakable chill still traveled through her from the inside outward. Delia turned from the computer as her body trembled. The muscle memory of Frank's torment haunted her. *Not again.*

"You need to leave, sir," Ginny snapped, sounding like Ken had no other alternative. Delia wished someday she could sound as confident.

"Delia needs to talk to me. Now!" Ken's voice boomed. "She fuck'n owes me an explanation!"

Her breath grew shallow. As she put her head between her knees, she heard yelling. Crashes. Then, the sound of shattering glass. *First Frank, now Ken.*

For a split second, the air went still before the shouting began again. But now, most of it came from Ginny.

Reaching across her desk, Delia grasped her phone. She locked her elbows enough to steady herself as she dialed 911. Sliding into the storage closet, she sat on the floor, making herself as small as possible as she frantically explained the situation to the dispatcher, who assured her the police were en route.

Flashbacks of her time at the Dragon danced through her head. Frank had humiliated her for much less. Ginny wouldn't tolerate this kind of thing. As much as Delia loved her job, and appreciated Ginny's patience as she grew into her role, she knew her time at Saint George's was about to end. *So much for this job.*

Bracing herself for the worst, she waited as she heard two new men's voices in the shop. Then, she heard Ken's voice again, whining, arguing, and eventually fading from the building.

Delia fumbled with the box on the shelf above her head until her fingers folded around a stray piece of tissue paper sticking out of a packing box. Her hand shaking, she grabbed it and used it to blot her face. As she reached for another piece, the closet door opened.

"You're safe," Ginny announced, extending her hand to Delia and pulling her to her feet. "He's been arrested. You okay?" She nodded and found everything around her moving in slow motion. Ginny continued, "From the expression on your face, I'd guess you recognized the voice?"

"It was my date Saturday night," Delia whispered. "I sent him a text and said I didn't think it would work out. I guess he was offended."

Ginny laughed, holding her Glock 19. "Well, he isn't one for rejection, is he?"

"I'm so sorry. I'll pay for anything he broke."

"Oh no. You didn't break anything. I guarantee he'll be paying for all the damages."

"Do you want me to clean out my locker?" Delia asked, her voice near cracking.

"Of course not! Christina will be back from lunch in a few. She'll be sorry she missed the excitement. We should have the shop cleaned up and running in no time."

Delia ran her hands through her hair, sighing. "I sure know how to pick them! Where do these men come from?"

Ginny patted Delia's shoulder. "I know it isn't any of my business, but I suspect you are attracted to these kinds of men."

"I swear to you, I'm not. I just want a nice guy who treats me right. Obviously, Ken isn't it." Delia said, "I . . . well, I guess I don't know how to find a good one."

"Maybe there are things you need to heal in your own life. Have you considered counseling?" Ginny said.

"Christina said something along those lines this morning."

"Christina knows what she's talking about. Listen to her if you won't listen to me."

"It isn't that simple," Delia muttered.

"Sweetie, if God wants you to fix something, there will be signs. It will be abundantly apparent," Ginny declared. "It will be like a neon billboard going off directly in front of you. You won't be able to miss it. But please! No more losers who show up in my store. Okay?"

***

Later in the afternoon, with the store's shelves upright, books back where they belonged, and the broken glass swept and disposed of, Delia returned to the computer in the back office. She pulled up one last online order for a customized baptismal cross, ordered by Allison Hayes in Tyler, Texas. The order form said the name to be engraved on it was, "Robert Patrick Wainwright."

Chapter Nineteen

The Discernment

"Hey, Paul. Got a minute?" Mitchell Ryan, the leader of the Stolen Voices meeting, said Monday night.

They stood under the awning of Saint Luke's Hospital. Paul zipped his jacket, keeping out East Texas's January weather. He looked around, ensuring he didn't recognize anyone. "Sure thing."

"Great observations you made in today's group," Mitchell said as they walked out of the building. "You seem to really get to the heart of the matter. I'm impressed. Are you a psychologist?"

"No, but my background is in counseling. Sometimes it seeps out," Paul said, shoving his hands into his pockets. "My master's thesis was on the impacts of abortion on men. Ironically, it was only a few months ago when I realized I still hadn't dealt with my grief."

"These men need to be heard. They come to this group filled with pain, shame, and heartache. You have a great understanding and compassion for their situation and have made a huge contribution to our group. You've been here what? Three months?"

"Something along those lines. Time flies, I guess."

"I hope they can someday hear your story," Mitchell said. "I'm not prying. I hope you feel comfortable enough to share at some point."

Paul knew at least three of the men in the group were Catholic. As a matter of recent frustration, Bishop Vance continued to discuss his upcoming clergy assignment, slated for next summer, offering him the opportunity to stay close to his siblings. Figuring his time with Stolen Voices needed to end before someone realized he was a priest, Paul hoped six months between his last meeting and his new parish assignment would be enough for the men to forget his face.

"I'm not going to share," Paul stated, as mental fleeting scenarios of Tyler's Catholic community carrying pitchforks and torches played out. "However, I assure you, being here has helped."

Mitchell took out his business card. "If you ever want to talk about what you've gone through, please reach out." He waited a beat then continued, "I don't know if this would interest you, but we have openings in our organization. We are always looking for men with your background. You're a natural leader. Something to think about, maybe?"

"Thank you," Paul said, taking the card, disappointed he'd been to his last meeting with the Stolen Voices group.

***

"I saw in the news Foster was sentenced to life," Morales said while eating breakfast at the Wagon Wheel a week later. "I was going to ask you how the trial went."

Paul took a bite of egg, chewed thoroughly, and wiped his mouth. Marvin Foster's trial had done nothing to improve his disposition. If he'd doubted his calling prior to sitting in the witness box while lawyers from both sides questioned Paul's memories from the night of the riot, afterward he had little doubt about the emptiness he felt for his vocation.

He shrugged. "It was uneventful. I was asked a few questions about what I saw. But I couldn't truly answer anything. When I came in, Armetta was dead."

"Are you satisfied with the verdict?"

"The jury didn't buy the self-defense argument, but I'm glad Foster's life was spared," Paul said.

"Have you gone to see him since the trial ended?"

"Associate Deputy Martinez expressly asked me to stay away from Ballentine Correctional. He had concerns. I can see his point. Armetta's friends aren't happy with the verdict. Foster just isn't happy and has shared this with his friends. Both sides want someone to blame."

"Looks like you won't be needing that prison ministry after all." Morales laughed. "God certainly does have a sense of humor, doesn't He?"

"Apparently He does," Paul agreed. "Let me ask you, Father, are you sure you want to stay here next week? You could go with the monsignor. I can hold down the fort."

Morales shook his head. "Oh no! Monsignor Costa specifically asked for you." Paul felt his face compress. "You truly are the best candidate for the job. With Father LeBlanc taking his vacation, he needs someone to fill in. Their friendship goes back decades. Costa has been the rent-a-priest there before. However, we both know the monsignor is getting up in years and can't handle a church that size on his own," Morales said. "There's what? Four weekend Masses plus daily Mass? More than two thousand parishioners? It is a far cry from our dinky country church in the middle of East Texas."

Paul lifted an eyebrow. "I was thinking, perhaps you might like a change of scenery. It might be nice for you to get away—"

Morales stuck out his hand. "Don't you try that with me. I know a *Tom Sawyer* move when I hear it. You go with Monsignor. You know the church, the staff, and the parish better than anyone. Consider it a calling."

Paul looked away, idly tapping his fingers on the table. Morales's words hung between them.

He studied Paul, giving him a knowing look. "Let me guess. You aren't ready to go back yet. You haven't gotten Shreveport out of your head, have you?" It was the most Morales said about the subject in months.

"No reason to dredge up old memories," Paul mumbled.

"So go make some new ones," Morales suggested. "When do you two leave?"

"Monday morning." Paul sighed. "You know, there are seminarians in Louisiana who could work with the monsignor. I could just drive him over, drop him off, perhaps."

"Like I said, God has a sense of humor. Maybe you aren't done with Shreveport." Morales drew back in his chair. "Any word on what parish the bishop is going to transfer you to?"

"I've asked to stay in Tyler or the surrounding area. I'd like to help my sister with her boys. Henry is her youngest. He'll be four in a month." Paul dipped his toast in his egg. "Bishop Vance has suggested a few parishes he'd like me to visit during Lent and see what I think."

"In my twenty-eight years in the clergy, I've never heard of a priest getting such preferential treatment on parish selection before. Especially one as young as you," Morales said.

"He's known me since I was a baby," Paul said. "He was my family's parish priest. My father was part of the Knights of Columbus and on the

Finance Council at our church. Mom taught religious education every Wednesday night."

"Still." Morales took a sip of his coffee.

"Is there something else?" Paul asked, pushing his plate back. "I've never been transferred before. I don't know how the process is supposed to work. You are saying this kind of transfer is highly unusual? I figured it was because I wasn't transferred a couple of years ago after Monsignor Costa's heart attack."

"It sounds more like he's trying to make sure you don't transfer to another diocese. After all, you did spend a lot of time in Louisiana last summer," Morales said. "But if you ask me, the bishop should have other concerns when it comes to you."

"Oh?" Paul raised an eyebrow. "What kinds of concerns?"

"It seems like it's a matter of time before you ask for laicization," Morales said. He let out a burst of laughter. "And from the look on your face, I'm going to say, I'm not far off."

Paul searched for the Wagon Wheel's single waitress. "Daisy, may I get a refill, please?" he asked, raising his coffee cup. Avoiding Morales's eye, he took a sip and wiped his lips with his napkin. Choosing his words, he asked, "What if I said you're right?"

Morales let out a snort. "I know I'm right."

"There's a lot to consider if I decide to leave the priesthood. I took a vow," Paul pointed out.

"God will know if you should have taken that vow," Morales said. "He understands."

"I haven't decided. I'm giving myself some time to discern if I want to leave," Paul said. "I need some time between uh . . . Shreveport . . . and any future decision I may make regarding my calling. I want to do God's will, not mine."

"Did I mention God has a sense of humor?" Morales asked.

***

Paul walked into the rectory kitchen after midnight Monday morning. He hoped to have a few solid hours of sleep before his drive with Monsignor to All Saints in a few hours. Just like every night for the past week, sleep escaped him.

Pouring himself a cup of milk and honey—his mother's tried and true sleep aid—he pushed the buttons on the microwave, wishing he had access to Costa's locked stash of alcohol to add a splash or two of Southern Comfort to his drink. However, he didn't have the nerve to tell the monsignor why he wanted the key to his liquor cabinet.

"If Jesus could only turn milk into whiskey," he grumbled.

Paul padded back to his room, passing Monsignor Costa's door. As his usual practice, he said a prayer for his mentor and friend. He added a few words for Father Morales as well, asking for strength and wisdom for him in his upcoming week alone at Saint Daniel's. As he turned toward his own room, a faint noise broke the silence.

Stopping, he listened for the sound again. From Costa's room, came a strangled gasp, then, "Father . . . help me."

Throwing open the door, he whipped on the overhead light. Monsignor lay on the floor, like an upended turtle clad only in cotton briefs. Reaching to him, Paul noticed Costa's sallow and clammy skin. The old man's glazed eyes looked beyond him, while his outstretched arm reached for something unknown and out of reach.

"Here, let me assist you," Paul said, rushing over to Costa.

He began lifting him to a seated position, realizing Costa had no strength to hold himself up. Grabbing a pillow, Paul propped his head atop while the monsignor made a guttural noise.

"Father Morales!" Paul shouted.

Morales, wearing green pajamas with his white hair shooting out in different directions, rushed into the bedroom. "Mercy!" he cried as he grabbed Costa's phone.

As Paul made the monsignor comfortable, Morales announced, "Paramedics are on their way."

Costa stared, his expression blank. His lips moved in a rhythmic motion, but no sound escaped. Paul and Morales exchanged a look, and in sync began praying over the monsignor.

With the noise of sirens nearby, Paul said to Morales, "Wait here, I'll go let the paramedics in."

He motioned to the first responders through the rectory. As he reentered the bedroom, Paul saw Morales pushing Costa's chest.

"Breathe," Morales commanded. "Breathe!"

The paramedics took over while he grabbed Morales's arm, moving him out of the way. Unable to speak, Paul jutted his chin toward the back wall, pulling the older priest with him. "He stopped breathing," Morales said in a hoarse whisper as a plaintive look spread across his face. "He wouldn't have wanted you to see that."

Time crawled while the two priests stood in the corner, as the first responders attempted to bring Costa back. They watched the movement of the paramedics and the undiscernible hubbub of activity all concentrated around the old priest lying on the carpet. After what seemed like hours but could have been mere minutes, he felt Morales's hand cup his shoulder as the truth became clear and time resumed its normal pace. Paul's second father figure just passed into Heaven.

Chapter Twenty

The News

"Heading out?" Morales asked Tuesday morning. He sat at the kitchen table as Paul rolled his suitcase across the linoleum.

"Considering Monsignor and I were supposed to be at All Saints yesterday . . ."

"Under the circumstances, I'm sure you can be forgiven," Morales conceded.

"Unless you'd rather go in my place. The offer's still open. I can stay here."

Morales shook his finger. "Oh no you don't. I'm not saying you will have an easier time. Think of it this way—may God forgive me for saying so—I'm stuck with hysterical weeping women grieving over our late pastor this week. They will expect me to comfort them as their tears flow all over the place. Would you rather go off to anonymity?"

"And may God forgive me for agreeing with you, but when you put it that way, I might have the better end of the deal."

Morales motioned toward the extra coffee cup. "But before you leave, come sit a moment. Enjoy a bit of morning alchemy and conversation. All Saints parish can be without their rent-a-priest a few minutes longer."

He shoved a plate of pastries in the direction of the coffee cup. "The congregation is already sending food. I can't eat this all myself."

"I'll take one for the road," Paul said but didn't reach for a muffin. "It's nice the community will be here for you while I'm gone. When my parents died, I lost twenty-five pounds in two months."

"The way the monsignor tells it, he said you were, how did he put it? 'A dumpster fire.'"

"Pretty accurate. I started summer school after their murders instead of taking time off. Like all twenty-year-olds, I thought I had everything under control." He glanced at Morales. "My longtime girlfriend and I were planning on getting married. I'd come back to Tyler to ask for my grandmother's engagement ring—it had been promised to me when I was ready. Instead . . ." Paul threw out a sardonic laugh. "My folks' funeral started late because we broke up right after I picked up Kayla from the airport. About a mile from the church, I made a U-turn and took her back to the terminal."

"Grief paints an interesting illusion, doesn't it?"

"Yeah . . . Monsignor arrived on my doorstep later that summer—Allison sent him. He slept on my couch. Hovered for a few weeks and—" Paul shook his head, lost in the memory of coming home from classes to see Costa, barefoot, wearing shorts and a t-shirt, cooking scrambled eggs and toast, slapping them on a plate while demanding he eat. "I brought him to basketball practice with me every day. Monsignor acted like he was around royalty instead of hanging out with a bunch of jocks on scholarship."

"The way he described it, his very reason for traveling to visit you was to watch the pre-season University of Arizona basketball camp." Morales shot a pretend basketball into the kitchen sink. His face grew serious. "He said you should have played professionally."

"No." Paul shook his head. "I played in college just because I wanted to. I thought I'd go into sports medicine. Life changes." He sipped his coffee. "Woah! What's this?"

Morales laughed and pointed to the bottle of Baileys. "The good monsignor left us his generous collection of libations. He couldn't take it with him." Lifting his cup, he said, "To Walter Costa. May the Lord welcome him with open arms!"

"Amen," Paul said, clinking his mug with Morales's.

"Monsignor also blamed himself—no, maybe more like regretted his words." He added more coffee to both mugs. "He told me he felt he pushed you into the priesthood."

"I knew I didn't want to be a doctor anymore." Paul rubbed his temples. "After my parents died, I wasn't sure what I wanted." He reached for the bottle of Bailey's, pouring into both cups, mumbling, "Maybe a little more . . . Monsignor offered me career advice. It was my choice to go to seminary."

"He told me more than once it was his deepest regret, thought he let you down," Morales stated. Paul jerked his head up, his eyebrows raised. "Monsignor said you were vulnerable at the time. He said he thought he pressed too much. He said you'd just as easily gone into rattlesnake wrangling if he suggested it."

"Possibly. But seminary took me four years. I committed. My own free will."

"Pride is the greatest of sins, Paul." Morales opened his mouth to continue, but he was interrupted by a loud knock on the rectory's kitchen door. Both men craned their necks across the room. "The grief-food parade has begun." He pushed his chair back from the table and strode through the kitchen. "We will need to have a potluck when you return. Invite your family," he said, opening the back door to greet a tear-stained woman who held a casserole dish in her hands.

***

Paul found the isolation away from Ballentine suffocating. Additionally, it seemed as if the All Saints' staff, including the associate pastor, used Father LeBlanc's absence as an opportunity for a work slowdown, leaving their rent-a-priest with the majority of the duties. Though he reasoned his job should have been a distraction, in reality, Costa's passing and the overwhelming responsibilities at All Saints did nothing but add to the notion already tap dancing in his head of how he should rethink his vocation.

Allison, whose sons were spending the week at their father's house, seemed to have some sort of sibling connection to his frustration. She'd called earlier in the day, offering to come to Shreveport for the weekend as his "emotional support twin." Paul considered, deciding between the massive workload at All Saints and Allison's inherent desire to smother him, he'd be better off on his own.

By Thursday night, Paul's need to break free from solitude and worship reached a volatile state. Even with all the opportunities for quiet reflection and stolen moments of prayer, he hadn't found a productive way to shut out his own destructive inner dialogue. After changing into his street clothes, he turned off his phone, hopped in his truck, and drove around looking for a sports bar.

"Please deliver me to Thy will and make your wishes abundantly clear," Paul prayed as he pulled into the parking lot, once again hoping God might listen.

"What'll it be?" the blonde behind the bar asked with a wink.

Paul sat back on the barstool admiring the woman's pale blue eyes. He didn't dare let his gaze drift beyond her face. "Sam Adams. I saw your special tonight was the cheeseburger. One of those. Everything on it and onion rings."

"You got it," she said, handing him his beer. "I'm Sheryl." She flashed him a smile. Pointing across the room she added. "I'm training a new waitress tonight. That's Susan. You need anything, get my attention. If I'm not behind the bar, grab her."

He motioned to the television behind her head. "All I need is the Mavericks game."

Sheryl leaned across the bar, her hair inches from his hands. "Sure. It's a shame you have to enjoy the game all by yourself."

Paul watched as she walked away. He caught her glance back at him through the mirror behind the bar while tossing her hair off her shoulder. Catching her eye, a shy grin crossed his face. She waved. He raised his bottle in her direction as her laughter reached his ears.

"Shreveport's a dangerous place," he muttered.

"Now, why's that?" a voice at his elbow said. Paul moved his head less than ten degrees to discover a pixie of a waitress putting a glass of water in front of him. She adjusted the pen behind her ear, causing the bits of her short auburn hair to stick out parallel to the ground. He gave her a questioning look. "You said Shreveport's dangerous. Just trying to figure out what you meant."

"Oh." Paul shook his head. "Sorry. Inside joke."

"No worries. I'm new. Trying to meet the regulars," she said but didn't budge. "I'm Susan."

"Paul. But I'm not a regular." He turned toward the game, hoping she'd take the hint and wishing he'd taken Allison up on her offer. His sister would've fended off the circling attractive women.

"Another beer?" Sheryl asked at halftime.

"I'd better stop. Susan—that was her name, right? She brought me water." He raised his glass. Not wanting Sheryl to leave, Paul asked, "How's she working out?"

"She's got a bit of job-PTSD. She worked at the Dragon Casino until Sunday. Huge raid."

"Dragon Casino? You don't say?" Paul squeaked while dribbling water on his face.

"Here." She dabbed his chin with a napkin.

He locked eyes with Sheryl while she bit her lip. In a deft move, Paul slid his hand down her arm, gently folding his fingers around her wrist. Her arm relaxed and her face spread into a smile. Grabbing the napkin and moving her hand from his face, he ignored the surge of energy radiating between them.

"I should tell you, I'm a Catholic priest," Paul said, still cradling her arm. "My ego loves the attention. Honestly, you're killing me, and not just because I'm a sucker for blue eyes and dimples. It's nice to be noticed by a beautiful woman."

She bristled for a beat and recovered. "Well, that sucks," Sheryl sighed, as she disentangled her wrist from Paul's hand. "Really, a priest? Or is it a nice brush-off? You're too cute to be a priest."

"Thanks." He pointed in the general direction of All Saints. "And yes. A priest. I'm helping at All Saints this weekend. Come on over for Mass."

Paul added, "Tell me about the raid at the Dragon. One of the parishioners worked there."

Sheryl, standing straighter now, waved to Susan. She jutted her chin in Paul's direction. "He wants to know about what happened at the Dragon," she said. "Can you fill him in?"

Susan shrugged. "The Dragon's operations manager was running an escort service out of the concierge desk for the casino's best customers." He felt her hand on his back. "Paul? You okay? You don't look too good."

"Yeah. Can I get more water? I need to work the beer out of my system," he whispered. Paul glanced at his napkin, which now seemed to be shredded into small bits of pulp. "So, everyone at the concierge desk was a prostitute?"

"Pretty much. We had two concierge departments. The regular concierge. You know, the one next to the front desk for most of the hotel's guests who want to know where the Cracker Barrel is located or those who needed help arranging for the airport shuttle. Then, there was the *Executive Concierge Desk* on the twelfth floor. This was for the casino's high rollers. Or, the 'special clients.' The ones who worked there called themselves 'escorts,' which was just a fancy word for whores. You following?" Susan asked as Sheryl put the fresh water in front of him.

"Yeah," Paul said, his voice hoarse.

He didn't dare pick up the glass, for fear of shattering it.

Susan continued, "Worst-kept secret around. Everyone who worked at the Dragon knew. I was a waitress in the bar. I wasn't about to do something so sleezy." She shuddered. "Never understood the chicks who did it. But I hear they made bank. Most of them worked there for years. One of them was even dating the operations manager *and* working as a hooker. Never understood those two at all. For years he beat the hell out of her then pimped her out. Messed up." She shook her head. "Anyway, big raid on Sunday night. The Dragon's been shut down until further notice."

Paul traced the rim of his water glass while studying the bar's varnished wood grain. Speaking in slow, short breaths he asked, "I'm guessing arrests?"

"Oh yes! The women involved and the operations manager—Frank Boudreaux, if you see him in the news. This was his department. I'm hearing he's going down for this. He's such an asshole. I hope he's locked up for a long time."

***

An hour later, Paul slammed the door of his truck, making the cab rock. His buzz now worn off, from time and from the bombshell Susan dropped. He'd spent the last half of the basketball game staring at his phone's screen, reading all he could about the Dragon raid. Anger boiled as he wrapped his head around an ugly truth.

Delia.

Paul thought about all she told him during their time together. Her life. Her job at the Dragon. At first, not wanting to rush or jump to conclusions, he decided perhaps he misunderstood. However, the more he researched, the more he knew the truth about her role at the Executive Concierge Desk.

Strumming his fingers on the dash, Paul sat in the parking lot, debating if he wanted to confront Delia. He knew the sensible course of action would be to let this part of his past go. After all, he had an impending laundry list of difficult items on his plate, including surviving his time at All Saints this week to giving one of next week's four eulogies at Monsignor's funeral.

Paul's priest training told him to forgive. Fill his heart with Christ's Peace and charitable love. However, nothing in the story he heard tonight—albeit secondhand—or his own thoughts warranted an easy forgiveness or anything resembling peace and love. Instead, anger played the predominant emotion, pulsing through him and radiating from his every pore.

Chapter Twenty-One

The Coincidence

Sunday morning, Delia drove to Mass at All Saints. With Father LeBlanc on vacation, she figured the substitute priest would preach a short, canned sermon. With any luck, she'd be in and out within an hour and able to get on with her day. Knowing what a horrible week Abigail had with the Dragon's raid and her arrest, Delia planned to check on her friend after church.

Since the weekend before, when Tawana called telling her to turn on the news, she'd thought of little else. With mixed emotions, Delia had sat glued to her television, watching the live telecast of the raid unfolding. Throughout the week, flashbacks of her life at the Dragon popped into her head. She recognized now how much her lack of self-worth and her desire to feel love through physical contact instead of through intimacy left her soul empty.

However, the knowledge she'd been nothing more than merchandise as if her subconscious hadn't fully processed what kind of broken person would sell their body, co-mingled with a spark of another, stronger thought. Delia found the power on her own to walk away from that life.

That emotional strength had carried her farther in a few months than in the eleven years she worked at the Dragon.

After Ken's outburst at Saint George's two months earlier, she took Ginny's and Christina's comments to heart. In the past few weeks, Delia unpacked much of her past with the help of her psychologist. Dr. Thompson helped her see how her lack of self-worth while working at the Dragon gave her the tendency to gravitate toward unfulfilling relationships. She now saw the pattern she'd created, not only with romantic partners but also with her work life at the casino.

Delia began focusing on creating a new path for her future. For the first time, she recognized an emotional strength in her thoughts and behaviors—a far cry from a year ago. She understood how much she owed Paul for bringing to light the dysfunction she'd lived with for so long, everything from her relationship with Frank to her time at the Dragon. Gratitude alone led her to draft him a letter. Someday, when the wording sounded correct, she'd send it to him at Saint Daniel's.

Through the process of her healing, Delia recognized a need to repair her spiritual life. At some point, she'd face this. But not yet. After all, if she couldn't send a simple letter to Paul, thanking him for directing her on to the right path, she didn't think she could face the Almighty. Telling Dr. Thompson her history proved to have been difficult enough, she couldn't imagine bringing her past to a priest through the sacrament of confession.

Arriving a few minutes before Mass, Delia entered the All Saints' vestibule. She glanced at her two favorite statues: Saint Gabriel blowing his horn, announcing the birth of Christ, and Saint Therese of Lisieux with her roses. Beelining to the holy water, she dipped her fingers in the bowl. As she crossed herself, she whispered, "Praise God, from whom all blessings flow."

Inside the crowded church, Delia found the group of women she sat with every week—left side, fourth pew from the back. Seeing them brought her a familiar comfort with the knowledge they had no idea about her past.

Christina moved over, making room for her while squeezing her arm. "Hi!" she said. "Saved you a seat."

Kneeling in the pew, Delia spent a moment in prayer. She expressed her gratitude and asked for guidance, concluding with her standard, "Your Will be done." But then, she added as a side note, "Whatever it might be, I'm ready." She caught herself, surprised at the new addition.

As the processional began, Delia stood, joining the congregation in singing *Gather Your People*. The altar servers carrying the candles came first, wearing their white robes. The younger of the boys seemed new, walking out of step. The other boy, a head taller, scowled while reaching over and slowing him down. After, came a seminarian, carrying a large metal cross, while singing too loud and off-key. Behind him trailed the deacon, holding the Gospel above his head. As he passed, Delia turned to the front, singing along with the congregation, paying little notice to the visiting priest, bringing up the rear.

Christina elbowed her. Leaning into Delia, she motioned with her thumb toward the priest's back. "I remember this guy from last summer. He came to All Saints a lot. I think he's from somewhere in Texas. Did you ever see him?"

Chapter Twenty-Two

The Broken

"Good to see you, Father Wainwright." Paul bristled as he turned toward the familiar voice. Delia sat on a stone bench in the garden next to the rectory parking lot, poised with her legs crossed and her hands clasped in her lap.

She rose, as her face relaxed into a smile. "Great homily today," she said, moving toward him. "You look cute in your priest clothes. My friend Christina calls you 'Father *Guapo*.'" With her arms outstretched, she reached for him. "How've you been?"

Paul threw up his hands while looking around to ensure they were alone. "Miss Hargrove, I believe the Catholic Daughters' lunch is in the parish hall." He jerked his thumb in the direction of the church. "This parking lot is for clergy and employees." Peeking at his phone, he calculated if he left now, he'd be at the sports bar in less than ten minutes. Plenty of time for the start of the Mavericks game. Clearing his throat he added, "Please excuse me. I have somewhere to be."

"Paul—"

"Look, I really don't want to talk."

"I heard about Walter Costa's death. Saint George's is handling the programs for the funeral. I saw you were speaking at the funeral Mass. He was your family friend? Your mentor? Right? *That* Walter?"

"Yes," Paul replied, clenching his jaw.

"My condolences. That must be tough."

Delia's fingers fluttered for his arm. Paul shifted his shoulder to the left, averting her hand. He shoved his fists into his pockets, squeezing them tighter. "Thank you."

"Paul," Delia began. "I've wanted to tell you. I'm sorry I acted so badly. You apologized and well . . . I can't believe I . . ." Catching his eye, she gave him a thin smile. "Well, I'm sorry. You deserved better than how I treated you that night."

Bitterness grabbed his jaw as he cast his glare at her. "You know what else I deserved?" Ice dripped from his voice as a no-nonsense expression spread across his face. "I deserved to know what you did for a living." Delia moved backward. He held up his index finger. "You kicked me out for the lie I told. Yet you couldn't be bothered to mention what happens at the Executive Concierge Desk. Not even once?"

She opened her mouth, letting a quiet gasp escape. "Paul, I—"

"And you know what else?" Paul asked, his voice lower. He thrust his extended finger toward her face. "I came clean before anything transpired. You didn't respect me enough to tell me the truth." Delia's mouth fell. He continued, "Don't look at me like you're shocked I found out. The raid's been all over the news this week." He glared. "I'm a priest. That's what I omitted. I wasn't the one selling my body and hanging out with you on the side."

She winced. "It wasn't like that."

All pretense of civility left Paul's voice. "Oh? From what I hear, it was exactly like that."

Delia's face grew taut. She stiffened her back. "I hardly think you are one to lecture me about lies," she said through clenched teeth.

Paul reached for his truck's handle. Opening the door, he snapped, "I'm not having this conversation."

***

"You know, if you weren't a priest, I'd swear you were hung up on a girl," Sheryl said an hour and a half later, handing him another beer. "I usually don't see that kind of look on a man unless there's a significant other."

Paul raised his bottle. "Cheers."

He took a long drink.

She reached across the bar, steadying his arm while catching his eye. "Slow down, Paul. Seriously."

He set the half-empty bottle down. "Water, please."

Sheryl patted his hand while moving the beer bottle out of his reach. "Sweetie, I'm cutting you off. For your own good." Sliding the water glass to him, she asked. "Want to talk about it?"

"Not really." He shook his head. "Lost someone special last week."

"Forgive me for saying so but aren't you religious folks supposed to be more . . ." she waved her fingers, "I don't know . . . Zen or something?"

Paul laughed. "I guess. Something like that."

Sheryl called to the man behind the bar as she hopped onto the stool next to Paul, "Raz, I'm taking a break."

Raz gave her a thumb's up.

"The one you lost? Tell me about her."

"Him," Paul said. He laughed at Sheryl's expression. "Nope. I like women—if that were an option for me—if that's what you're thinking."

"I was confused for a minute. I was pretty sure you made that clear the other night."

"He was my godfather. My father's best friend. The uncle who wasn't an uncle. That kind of guy." Paul cast his gaze downward. "Died suddenly last week. He was the one who saved me from myself when I didn't have it in me to go on."

Sheryl placed her hand on Paul's shoulder. "You know he's still with you. Right?"

Paul gave her a half smile. "Yeah. It was just . . ." He groaned. "I wish I would have been straight with him before he passed. He asked me if I had a gambling problem." Paul scoffed. "Truth was, no I don't gamble. And I told him so." He shook his head and took another sip of water.

"Sounds like you were straight with him," she pointed out.

"I was doing worse." He eyed her. "Well, worse by priest standards." Sighing, he added, "I didn't want him to be disappointed in me, so I let him think I was lying to him. A sin by omission." Paul looked away. "He would have done anything for me. He *did* everything for me. And I didn't give him the courtesy of the truth."

Sheryl said, "I'm no religious expert, but aren't you all supposed to agree you're imperfect and kind of accept each other's imperfections?"

He played with the rim of his glass. "That's a simplistic way to explain it. I just wish I could go back and confess how *imperfect* I was."

She leaned back. "You know, in my line of work, I see a lot of folks who think they are hiding the truth from others. But in reality, those other people have known what's been going on for a long time and figure the truth will come to light sooner or later." Paul met her eyes. "Maybe your friend might have been that way, too. He might have known what you weren't willing to admit. He might have figured when you were ready to talk about it would be the time when you were ready to make some changes."

***

"Thank you for meeting me," Paul said as they stood in the parking lot of Mama Maria's Tacos Monday afternoon. "I'm sorry about yesterday. I shouldn't have—"

Delia made a dismissive motion with her hand. "Don't worry about it." She crossed her arms. "I'm not hungry and I only have an hour for lunch. What about you? Do you want to eat?"

"Not particularly. Let's just walk." Paul waved to the staff in the red ramshackle building next to the Red River, again wondering if Divine intervention held up the structure. He and Delia found Mama Maria's Tacos last summer, where they became regulars. The place lacked ambiance and the only seating happened to be three concrete picnic tables under a tin awning, overlooking the parking lot of the boat launch. The delicious food and friendly staff more than made up for the building's faults.

He led, winding them toward the boat launch, along the river—a short quarter mile away. Stealing a glance, Paul took in Delia's features. She appeared more weathered around the eyes, as if the last five months had aged her more than the hard living she'd done in the past several years. But more than that, to his amazement, the halo he'd envisioned crowning her head seemed to have vanished.

Even with the rift between them, he found the unfamiliar quiet unsettling. "You know," Paul started, "there are certain health-related implications . . ."

Delia groaned. "*That's* the direction you want to take this conversation?" She rolled her eyes as she plodded on the path. Raising her hands, she said, "I'm clean. Okay? I had blood tests every month. I still do—just in case."

"You should have told me," he blurted. "I had a right to know."

She tightened her jaw as she turned, facing Paul. "Let's get something straight. You need to get off your pious soapbox. If I'd told you the first time we met—when I had the flat tire—that I was a high-class escort, would you have wanted to be friends?" She flipped her hands into the air. "Let me guess. Nope. You probably wouldn't have paid for my Uber, let alone my tire. You wouldn't have given me a second look."

Paul gave a humorless laugh. "Let me stop you right there. Yes. I would have."

She narrowed her eyes. "Okay, Paul. Would you have invited me to lunch?"

"Believe it or not, I guarantee I would have invited you to lunch."

Delia's voice rose. "Why? So you could change me? Judge me? Pretty self-righteous, don't you think?"

Paul raised an eyebrow. "It's not self-righteous at all." He shook his head. "But my motivation would have been different. If I knew upfront you were selling your body, I still would have invited you to lunch because I would have wanted to see if you needed help. I would have asked you if you were happy with—what did you call yourself? An 'escort.' If you weren't happy, I would have asked what I could have done to help you get out of that life. Because that's what I am called to do. It is my vocation to help save souls."

He frowned. "So, let me ask you, were you happy with your job? Did you *want* that life? You didn't seem in any hurry to quit

until . . ."

She pointed a finger at him. "But I did quit. I quit before anything happened between us."

"Here's where I'm lost, Delia. You still lied to me. I have no reason to believe you wouldn't have kept lying to me."

Jamming her hands on her hips, Delia scoffed. "You can't do what-if scenarios. That's not fair. We both lied." She threw up her hands. "I got news for you. Neither of us were saints."

Paul opened his mouth to reply. Instead, her comment elicited a momentary chuckle. "You're right about that," he said, shaking his head. "We weren't. Not by a long shot."

She sighed. "Paul, you're right. I lied to you. And I'm sorry. I was wrong. I should have told you. The truth was ugly. I wasn't ready to admit it to myself at the time." She looked away. "I didn't know how to leave the Dragon. I met you and I thought you'd be that white knight in shining armor who'd come in and save me." She gave a whispered laugh. "But you didn't rescue me. Okay? You showed me a better path and I found my own strength. I owe you a lot for that. Thank you."

"I'm happy for you. I really am." Paul held her gaze while his fond memories of their time last summer played in his head. His cautionary voices nudged him, bringing him to the present, but not before the faint scent of vanilla perfume reached his nose. Delia turned toward the Red River. He watched a paddle wheeler float by, listening to the muffled laughter of its passengers. "Remember when we took that tour?" he asked, pointing to the boat as the tension of the moment left him.

"Yes, I do. It was a lot of fun. Independence Day. We sang goofy little kid songs as we drove back to my place." She laughed. "It was hot that day. I thought I was going to melt on that boat."

"I liked it. I had a great time." Paul smiled. "I had an excuse to stand close to you. I was always looking for excuses." His voice grew soft. "I'm actually curious. How did you get into something like this? I mean, why? Delia, you are such a smart and talented woman. You are so giving and caring. You have so much to offer this world. How did the amazing and confident person I met make those choices?"

"I didn't know what else to do. I didn't know how to quit. Or at least that's what I told myself," Delia mumbled. "I was nineteen when I moved to Shreveport. I was waiting tables. Frank would come in. He flirted, made me feel special in a way only one other man ever made me feel special . . ." She bit her lip as she nudged him. Paul felt his cheeks flush. "The difference was that Frank had ulterior motives. He was the Dragon's operations manager. I was living with him before two months went by. He even gave me money to send back to Mama to help her out. I thought this was what adult life was like."

"But you were living with Frank? Did he expect you to be his girlfriend *and* work as a—"

Delia nodded. "Oh, he did."

"He *groomed* you?" Paul gasped.

"Pretty much," Delia conceded. She shrugged. "Frank always told me sex was the only thing I was good at. And once I started working at the Executive Concierge Desk, he said nobody else would want me." She faced Paul. "The money at the Dragon was good. I was able to help my family. Mama had cancer and no insurance. Tommy helped, too, but he couldn't do it himself. Frank offered Maddy a job when she graduated from high school. I pushed so hard for her to go to college because it terrified me to think she'd come to Shreveport . . . I didn't want this for her." She shook her head. "But then again, I wanted to make sure they were taken care of. It might sound silly, but it was a badge of honor to be able to help them out. I came from nothing, and I made the highlife. At least I thought I did."

She eyed him. "I don't expect you to understand. You don't have a past."

"We'll have to agree to disagree on my lack of a past," Paul muttered.

A gust of wind blew across the river. Delia brought her arms to her body as armor against the cold.

Paul shrugged off his jacket, wrapping it around her shoulders. "Your sweater is a little thin for January."

"Thank you." Delia pulled the jacket tighter.

He asked, "If I told you I was a priest, would you have had lunch with me?"

She snorted. "Of course. But I wouldn't have expected us to become friends. I would have figured you were another unavailable lonely guy looking for something short-term."

He chuckled. "I guess I was."

Delia pointed at him. "That's what I specialized in."

"What about now? Do you specialize in *that* kind of man?"

"Who's asking? Paul Wainwright or Father Wainwright?" She nudged him.

He nudged her back, enjoying the familiarity. "Both."

"No. I don't. Funny you should ask. I've been seeing a counselor who's helping me work through why I sought out unhealthy relationships. Of course, I thought *you* were a healthy relationship." She added, "Since I left the Dragon, I've realized significance is a greater value than success. I've learned a lot about myself. Keep in mind, I still have some cleaning up to do. I haven't found my way to confession—baby steps. But I'm not that woman you knew in August."

"Yeah. I guess we both were lost."

"Why were you . . ."

"Interested in you?" Paul supplied.

She raised one shoulder. "Pretty much."

He sighed. "For a while, I'd been deciding if I wanted to stay in the priesthood. I went in for the wrong reasons. Priests usually have what is known as 'the calling,' which is like an unmistakable message from God." He chuckled. "I assure you, that's not what happened. In my case, I told God what I was going to do instead of asking God what He wanted me to do."

He stopped, mid-step, debating how to continue.

"If you don't want to talk about it—"

"It's . . . It's okay." Paul shook his head. "When I was twenty, Kayla and I had been living together for a couple of years when she got pregnant. She wanted to keep the baby a secret, so we hadn't told anyone yet. At the time I was under the impression it was because she wanted to surprise our families. When she was five months along, we went to the women's clinic on campus for her ultrasound.

"Kayla wouldn't look at the monitor, instead she kept her eyes closed the entire time. But I kept staring at that little person. We found out we were having a boy. I saw the heartbeat—his fingers and toes." Paul stopped walking. His voice cracked. "He was sucking his thumb inside the womb. Plain as day."

"If this is too personal, I understand," Delia said.

He felt the heartache grow through his chest. Shaking his head, Paul said, "No. It's fine. During the ultrasound, Kayla kept saying, 'This can't be real.' I didn't catch on at first because I was self-absorbed in my excitement. I was going to be a father. I mean, how could anyone not be excited after seeing their child sucking their thumb? The little heartbeat?" He closed his eyes. "Later that day I discovered she had other plans."

Even after listening to the men at the Stolen Voices group for the last several months, the pain still stung as if it happened yesterday. "I thought I talked her out of it. I thought we were on the same page. So, I went back to Tyler to see my folks. She rode with me to Albuquerque where I dropped her off at her aunt's house."

He wiped his hand across his lips as his voice cracked. "Did you know abortion is legal until birth in New Mexico? I didn't then." Paul bent down, his head in his hands. His voice trailed off as he shared the rest of the nightmare he endured. "I got back to my parents' home in Tyler the next night. I knew they were expecting me. I'd been calling on and off all day and nobody answered . . . I found out why. Dad was by the front door." He closed his eyes as he worked to get the image out of his mind. "Mom . . . I found her on the kitchen floor. There were three of them. Ex-cons, caught by DNA evidence. One is now serving two life sentences in a penitentiary outside of Dallas, and another is locked up outside of Houston. The last guy was sent to a maximum-security prison in Oklahoma."

"Oh, Paul! I'm so sorry." Delia gasped, throwing her hands to her mouth. "I never realized your parents were murdered. I don't know what to say."

"Allison has generously pointed out how I blamed myself for all of their deaths." He shrugged. "She's right. I thought I could make it up to God."

"Your son. Your parents. None of this was your fault. It seems like a lot to be carrying around all this time."

"I'd buried it," he said. "Then the riot happened."

"Riot?"

Paul whipped his head toward Delia. "I never told you? That was the fourth death to my name. At least at the time, I thought it was."

Chapter Twenty-Three

The Healing

"Hello, Father," Delia said, hoping she came across as a confident professional, while she watched Paul, who was wearing a black shirt and his priest collar, enter Saint George's Books Wednesday afternoon. She waved toward the three taped boxes on the counter. "I have these ready for you."

"Happy to help . . ." He squinted at her nametag. "Delia."

"Here," she said, making an exaggerated effort to suggest the box had weight. "Let me take the last one." Delia called over her shoulder as she walked out Saint George's shop door, "Christina, I'm going to lunch. Will you tell Ginny?"

"Can do," Christina said. She didn't look up from unpacking a new shipment of books.

Last night, at her weekly counseling appointment, they discussed Delia's challenges in moving on from certain aspects of her past. This didn't just include Paul, but also everything the Dragon represented in her adult life.

Delia felt she needed to release her shame and guilt and look toward a brighter future. But how? For an hour, they reviewed various beneficial strategies. One of the ideas Dr. Thompson threw out included taking the opportunity while Paul was still in Shreveport to "complete" their relationship.

"Complete," as Delia explained, sounded like a New Age term and it was a little too hocus-pocus for her Southern upbringing. Dr. Thompson suggested she overlook the name and concentrate on the activity, which consisted of saying to Paul whatever she needed to say and allowing him to do the same so they could part as friends. Though Delia argued that they had done this Monday afternoon, her psychologist asked her to use the opportunity of returning his jacket as a dry run for other areas where she might need "completion" in the future.

From there, a seed of an idea began to grow. However, she opted not to mention it during her session. Instead, as soon as she left Dr. Thompson's office, she texted Paul, asking him to come by Saint George's.

"I'm not sure Saint Daniel's needs this many bottles of altar wine," Paul stated, eyeing the writing on the side of the box. "Plus, I've lifted altar wine boxes before. Aren't they usually heavier?"

"Much heavier. These are empty. Sorry for the ruse. I didn't want to draw attention . . . if you know what I mean." She chuckled. "Figured nobody at my work needed to know why I had your jacket."

"Your hair," Paul said as they placed the boxes in the back of his truck. He moved his fingers toward her head, pausing in midair, his hand momentarily suspended before he tucked a lock behind her ear. "It's . . . nice."

"It was time for a new look." Delia twisted that same errant strand around her finger, which made it fall on her cheek a second time. "Shorter than it's ever been."

"You look sophisticated."

"I think that was a compliment."

"It was," he said. "Though I like long hair on women. Just a preference."

"On the women you date?" Delia gasped, horrified Paul would be offended by her joke. She nudged his shoulder hoping it conveyed her sentiment.

Paul tilted his head upward, laughing. "Yes. Something like that." He smiled at Delia with an expression of friendship and nudged back.

"You parked next to me. Great." Delia reached inside her car. "Here you go. I appreciated the loan. Thanks. I was really cold Sunday." She briefly pulled the jacket back, away from Paul's outstretched hand, inhaled it, and then passed it to him. "I just wanted a moment . . . Don't laugh. It smells like you."

Paul rocked back on his heels. "I'm honored. Why don't you keep it? Something to remember me by. You can pull it out of your closet ten years from now and say, 'Oh yeah . . . that priest guy.'"

"Now, now . . . Do you really think I would forget you, Mr. Wainwright?"

"I'd like to think I made a lasting impression." He winked. "Plus, I'd like to be a fly on the wall when your latest boyfriend sees it and wonders where the jacket came from."

"There's no 'latest boyfriend.'" Delia waved her hand. "Yes, I can see by that smile, you approve of that decision." He waggled his eyebrows. "I decided a couple of months ago to take a break from men. I need to learn a few things about myself. It was also time to learn a few things about self-love and forgiveness."

"Sounds very healthy," Paul stated. "I've given that same advice to people who've come to me for counseling. Of course, they were involved with folks under different circumstances—at least I hope they were."

She lowered her eyelids. "You know, that last boyfriend of mine. He's the one who took me for a tailspin. Made me rethink my life choices."

"I know what you mean, I met this incredible woman once who made me forget myself."

Delia relaxed, appreciating the ease of their conversation. "Please don't take this wrong. Paul, why are you a priest?"

He raised an eyebrow. "You sound like Allison."

"I wish I could have met her," Delia replied, now clutching Paul's jacket. "I bet she's a hoot. But you didn't answer my question. I don't mean because of us," she gestured between them, "but because I guess, I'm not hearing that you got the calling."

He put up his palm. "Truly, stop talking like my sister."

"I just wonder, for your sake, if you've been tempted before, don't you think it could happen again?"

"There won't be a next time. I learned my lesson. I don't want to hurt the ones I love."

Delia rose on her toes, planting a kiss on Paul's cheek. "You're a good man, Mr. Wainwright."

"And you are pretty special yourself," Paul replied. He paused, and Delia thought he might say more. Instead, he looked at his watch. "I have to run. We have the viewing tonight for Monsignor Costa in Tyler. I need to get there by four. Tomorrow's the funeral. I still need to put the final touches on my part of the eulogy."

"Paul." Delia's voice grew somber as she gazed off into the distance. She twisted her fingers. "There's something I'd like to ask before you go. It's a big favor."

"Of course."

She studied a small crack in the asphalt. "It's, well . . . I have behaved badly in my adult life. I'm not that person anymore. I need to put that behind me. I'm ready to move on."

"I know you are," he said. "I assure you, that's obvious. You've changed. It shows. You are a better woman for it."

"But . . . I haven't . . . Never mind . . . It isn't important, I'm sorry I brought it up. I don't—"

"Delia." Paul placed his hand on her arm. He waited until he caught her eye before he asked, "What's going on? How can I help you?"

"I want to do something I haven't done since I was a kid. It's been a long time. This is awkward. But if you wouldn't mind . . ." She inhaled a deep breath while letting her brain catch up with her babbling. She blurted, "Father, will you hear my confession?"

"Oh." Paul stepped back. "I . . . I wasn't expecting that."

She shook her head. "It's . . . I'm sorry. I should just find another priest. I just thought . . . well, I don't know what I thought."

Paul opened his truck's passenger side door. She watched him rummage through his suitcase.

"Did I offend you?" she asked, cupping her hands to her mouth. "Oh, Paul, I feel like I screwed things up between us again. Honestly, I don't want things to be weird."

Popping his head back out of the cab, he held a rolled strip of cloth in his hand. "It's never a problem. This is my job. I specialize in saving souls. Plus, I have a vested interest in *your* soul and if you are ready for reconciliation, then I'm duty bound." With a flick of the wrist, he unwound a long silky scarf. "My stole. For such occasions."

"Reconciliation?"

"A fancy word for confession. That's what it's called. It has been a long time, hasn't it?" Paul nudged her shoulder.

Delia giggled. "You look so official. Look, you may not like me when I'm done."

"Christ has given me the authority to forgive. John, chapter 20, as I'm sure you recall from my fabulous homily last Sunday."

She glanced at him, grateful for Paul's playful nature putting her at ease.

He continued. "Hearing confessions is part of my job. Salvation is my goal. You know I can never discuss—even with you—what I hear without your permission. But I assure you, your past doesn't define you. And, I will still like you." Paul paused and shook his head. "But you know, this is slightly . . . unusual. God knows what is in your heart. He knows what you are sorry for. There's no reason to go into finite detail about your past sins. You can be general, as long as you are truly ready to repent."

"Oh, that's good. I was starting to think . . . what if I had to state every past . . . um . . . shall we say, offense?"

She watched the color drain from Paul's cheeks. Swallowing, he turned and opened his cab again, this time pulling out a blanket from behind the front seat. "This way," he said, motioning for Delia to follow him to the back of the truck. Opening the tailgate, he smoothed out the blanket on the bed's cold metal.

"Thank you, Father," Delia murmured.

"Let me ask you, do you want to look at me, or would you like me to turn my back?"

She sighed, "Does it matter at this point?"

"I'll just sit next to you. When I hear confessions, I often close my eyes. So, don't be surprised by that." Paul added, his voice serious, "Please, take your time and think about everything you are confessing. Get your thoughts together."

"You might hear some things."

"It's okay. I'd bet I've heard worse. But don't feel a need to be specific. God understands better than I do."

"Do you always tell people to keep their confessions general? Or am I just special?" She poked his shoulder.

Paul raised an eyebrow. "Let's put it this way, I've confessed my past. I've moved on and repented. I've atoned for my sins. Would *you* want to hear my past sins in great detail?"

She nodded. "I see your point."

Delia slipped on Paul's jacket and pulled it close to her. "Do I have to confess about you? I mean about that almost-night—because I have to tell you . . ." She fanned herself and batted her eyelashes. "Never have I ever, Mr. Wainwright."

Deep crimson crept up his face. "If you feel a commandment was broken, or your actions might have been offensive to God, then yes. If you need to lump it into one big category, that's fine."

"Did *you* feel a commandment was broken?"

"You need to decide for yourself. But yes, I went to confession," Paul said, hopping onto the tailgate.

She scanned the parking lot. "I didn't think this through, but I'm kind of glad we aren't in direct sight of Saint George's front door." She frowned. "Don't really want to be interrupted or have to answer any questions from Ginny or Christina."

"We can go somewhere else." Paul extended his thumb over his shoulder. "Inside the truck?"

"No. I want to do this. Before I lose my nerve. Besides, I'm sure they'd understand. They're Catholic. I mean, I would if I saw them talking to you."

He patted the space beside him while placing his stole around his shoulders. "Have a seat in my confessional, Ms. Hargrove."

Delia settled onto the truck bed. Reaching for him, she squeezed his palm. The nervous energy she'd been experiencing washed away, replaced by an instantaneous calm. "Thank you, Paul." Then placing her hand to her forehead, then to her chest, and then touching both shoulders, she said, "Bless me, Father, for I have sinned."

Chapter Twenty-Four

The Decision

"Leftovers! Funerals are great for free food," Allison announced Thursday afternoon as they walked in her door. She grabbed the foil pans filled with leftover casseroles from Chuck's hands. Kicking off her heels she said, "Britt, Thanks for watching the boys." Looking out the window, she hollered, "Archie, put that stick down! Do not hurt your brother!" She turned to Paul. "Great eulogy, by the way."

"Thanks," Paul said, setting his leftover food containers on her counter. He peeked underneath the top one, pleased to find a pasta dish. Turning toward Brittany, he stretched out his arms. "May I?" he asked, taking Robert.

Sliding into a kitchen chair, he snuggled with Robert. "Monsignor had an inspiring life. I'm blessed to have known him."

"Agreed," Allison said. "How many times did he get you two out of trouble?"

"Countless. Let's just call him what he was: a miracle worker. Patient, too. He had to be to deal with the Wainwright boys. But yes, Monsignor was an amazing man," replied Chuck. "Great basketball coach, too."

"We wouldn't have gone to All-State without him coaching us in high school," Paul replied.

"You wouldn't have played for the University of Arizona at all without him," Chuck corrected.

Brittany changed the subject. "You're a natural with the baby, Paul. Want to babysit?"

"Sure. When do you guys want to go out?"

"You aren't going to have much time now that Saint Daniel's is down a priest," Allison pointed out.

"There's time," Paul said as Robert played with his hair. He cleared his throat. "I won't be at Saint Daniel's much longer."

"Did you get your transfer to Tyler?" Chuck asked, his head inside the refrigerator. He handed Brittany a Diet Coke and set one of the two beer bottles he had in his hand next to Paul before flopping on a kitchen chair.

Paul looked at the three. "Actually, I'm meeting with Bishop Vance tomorrow. I'm going to petition for laicization."

Chuck sighed and whipped out his wallet. "I was ready this time." He shoved a stash of bills into Allison's outstretched hand. Glaring at Paul he growled, "If you rigged this, I'm gonna kick your ass."

"Rigged?" Paul asked.

"I bet Chuck fifty it would be less than a week from Monsignor's funeral before you bailed." Allison shrugged. "To be fair, Chuck said at least a month."

"Any other bets you two have on my behalf?"

"Yes," they replied in unison.

Paul gestured to Chuck. "If you split the pot with me, I'll help you win. We can stick it to Allison."

"Oh Paulie, we've been betting on you for years." Allison waved her hand around the kitchen. "How do you think I paid for this remodel?"

"Chuck, really, let me know if you want help."

"Seriously Chuck!" Brittany snapped. "Take the help." She looked at Paul. "What is that word you just used that cost my family fifty bucks?"

"It means I'm leaving the priesthood," Paul replied.

"Really? How exactly does that work?" Brittany asked.

"Well, I have some paperwork to fill out. I must give reasons. The paperwork is processed all the way to Rome."

"What happens though?" Chuck asked. "Once you fill out the forms, do you still do your priestly duties?"

"At some point, I will be asked to stop. It might be as early as me turning everything in that I go on administrative leave. At that time, I'll have to move out of the rectory." He looked at his brother and sister. "Which one of you loves me enough to have me be your built-in nanny while I sleep on your couch?"

"Dibs!" Allison said, waving her hand while bouncing on the balls of her feet. Looking at Brittany she added, "Bring Robert over here, Paulie won't mind watching a fourth kid."

"What do you plan on doing?" Brittany asked.

Paul shrugged. "One thing at a time. If nothing else, I can take my boards and become a clinical psychologist. But I don't know if that is what I want to do."

"Well, Ally doesn't make it look glamorous," Chuck pointed out.

"It's more like I feel like I've already done plenty of counseling," Paul said. Maybe I need a complete change of vocation. With my master's I can teach. Tyler has a few colleges. But I'd still need to find something sooner."

"If you need money, Bro . . ." Chuck said.

"I have money saved. Our inheritance, after all. I'm thinking of daily living expenses. At some point, I'd like to officially start dating."

"Anyone in particular?" Allison asked.

"Not sure."

Brittany, who had been filled in on Delia, asked, "Weren't you in Shreveport for the past week?"

"I was. Worked at All Saints," he conceded. "But my decision to leave had been weighing on me long before that." He looked at their three staring faces. Paul rolled his eyes. "And yes, I did see Delia. Okay?"

"And?" Allison and Brittany asked together.

"Nothing really. We both have unfinished business. I hope that door is open or at the very least, unlocked. But she told me some pretty heavy things I need to process. I'm not sure how I feel about that."

"You know," Brittany started. "You did a great job on the nursery. I love Robert's crib. Have you thought about being a handyman?"

Paul laughed, "No, I hadn't, but I have a few skills. Maybe."

Allison's face lit up. "I have a job for you. It pays my undying love. But you know, it would be a perfect project." She tugged Paul's arm, leading him toward the kitchen door. "Come with me."

They stood at the back of the property looking into Allison's shed. "I never use this space. I'd been thinking about turning this into an apartment and renting it out. If I bought the supplies, would you be interested in converting this for me?"

"Great idea, Ally," Chuck said. "You've got a sink in that corner and obviously there's electricity. You probably would want someone with better skills than Paulie to run the line for a toilet. But I could see this working."

"And then you'd have your own place until you get on your feet," Allison said.

"Now wait a sec, Allison, I'm a priest, not a miracle worker. This place . . ." he looked around at the building that made Mama Maria's Tacos look like a palace. "It needs a lot of help."

"God will show you the way. I have faith," Allison said, patting his shoulder. "I'll call the city tomorrow and get the permits. Then I'll call a plumber."

***

"How did it go?" Father Morales asked Friday afternoon as Paul walked into the Saint Daniel's office carrying a thick packet of paper.

"If I told you Bishop Vance wasn't surprised, what would you say?" Paul asked.

"I'd say that the only surprise would be why it took you so long?"

"The bishop asked me something along those lines. Like I told him, I made a vow. Going back on a promise to God isn't the same thing as welching on a bet," Paul said.

"We have a loving God. He knows your heart. He also knows that you have put more thought into leaving than you did into actually going into the priesthood. I suspect if God wants you to stay, you will know."

"The process isn't simple. I have to go to counseling. There's a retreat somewhere—"

Morales clasped his hands. "Praise God! Finally! You are taking a vacation."

"Not exactly, I'm supposed to spend a couple of weeks living in silence, at an Abbey, reflecting. I plan on taking that seriously. The bishop is either sending me to an Abbey in Kansas City or Biloxi, Mississippi. Given the weather Missouri is having this winter, I'm hoping for Mississippi."

"Any idea when that's supposed to happen?"

"He had his assistant look for a rent-a-priest while I was meeting with him. I think Father Kunkle is coming in from Mount Pleasant next week. So, it looks like I'm heading out sooner than later."

Morales reached into a cabinet behind his desk and came out with a bottle of amaretto and two coffee cups. "We may thank the monsignor for another of his donations," he said as he poured. "You know, I find that men who have been in a position of high authority with God often have a hard time learning the humility that might need to come with this kind of life change."

"Are you concerned about me?" Paul asked.

He shook his head. "You? No. But I felt compelled to warn you, the world doesn't see you as holy as you might see yourself."

"I'm not sure I ever saw myself as 'holy.'" Paul shook his head. "I promise, if my ego gets out of hand, I'll come to you first." He passed the stack of papers to Morales. "Once I put my petition in, I will be relieved of my duties. I have to give evidence that at the time I was committed to be ordained, I was unfit to make that decision."

"How do you think that will play out?"

He took off his glasses, cleaning them on the edge of his shirt. "I can justify that. My parents passed. I had . . . other reasons as well. I don't regret becoming a priest and I'll always be proud of the work I've done. But a choice made from grief and guilt isn't a true calling. I didn't come into this for the right reasons."

Morales asked, "Have you lost your faith?"

Paul shook his head. "No. In fact, as I have been discerning, I see my faith strengthening. I just need to focus it in another direction."

"Shreveport?" Morales asked.

Paul shrugged. "Not exactly, maybe in the future, there might be some additional 'Shreveport.' I want to marry. Whether it's with anyone in Shreveport or not remains to be seen." It was the most Paul had admitted to Morales about his indiscretions the summer before. "But I am not leaving the clergy for a woman."

Morales said, "Paul, if you want to leave, you don't have to jump through these hoops. Just walk away. After so many years, the bishop can automatically grant you laicization." He threw up his hands, scoffing. "The entire situation is ridiculous, actually! If the Church would just drop its Victorian view that sexual activity is somehow unbefitting of men of the cloth. After all, if it can be part of a sacrament of marriage . . .

"Falling in love is human and natural for any man, and that includes priests. Progressing with a relationship of love is natural and normal and the Will of God. If you think about it, it was God's first directive, 'Go forth and multiply.' It's the hierarchy in the Church who thinks otherwise. The Church docs this to themselves."

Morales shook his head. "Listen to me go on and on—"

"You seem to have strong opinions," observed Paul.

"You have no idea," Morales said. "God can ask a man to serve Him and provide him a wife. It isn't a mutually exclusive idea."

Paul said, "That's not why I'm leaving."

Morales emptied his glass and poured another one, topping off Paul's as well. "Maybe not, but that's the outcome you desire once you are free."

"True."

"Did you ever think about it? In any other set of teachings, mandated celibacy would be considered brainwashing. This is what cults do to control their people. Plus, it does not reflect Scripture and God's ultimate plan for man and woman. But priests! They blindly agree to these rules. Honestly, it's time some of them began to question this hypocrisy. Celibacy is a noble calling if a man is truly called. But it should be the *man's* choice, not the Church's."

"Why did you agree to this life?" Paul asked.

Morales raised an eyebrow. "Who says I did? I live through Scripture. I will allow Him alone to be my judge."

Chapter Twenty-Five

The Beginning

"Good to see you!" Paul said.

"You too," Delia replied, leaning in for a hug. "It's been too long. What? Five months?"

Paul embraced her while inhaling her familiar vanilla perfume. As he pulled back, he let his hands slide down her arms. His fingers intertwined with hers. "I've missed you."

A honk came from across the street, breaking the moment. Father Morales stepped out of the Saint Daniel's parish car, holding two gift bags. A broad grin spread across his face. Paul dropped Delia's hands and offered a hesitant wave.

Morales threw back his head and let out a belly laugh.

"Great to see you, Paul. You look good. Dare I say, happier than I've seen you in a long time." Morales began walking toward the Camry, a smirk plastered across his face. He stuck out his hand to Delia. "Alejandro Morales."

"Oh!" Delia exclaimed. "*You're* Father Morales!" She let her fingers flutter into Morales's hand. "I'm Delia. A friend of Paul's."

"Shreveport?" Morales asked with an eyebrow raised.

Paul gave his head a half tilt.

"Monsignor would have approved," Morales said, clapping Paul's shoulder. "It appears the two of you need a few minutes to become reacquainted. I'm going to go inside where the beer and gossip will freely flow. Your family can fill me in on anything I need to know. If not, I will be happy to provide any details they don't have."

"Nice to meet you!" Delia said.

"I'll report to them that you are quite the catch, too," Morales offered. "That way they won't have to gawk out the window."

"Appreciate that," Paul replied.

Morales waved as he walked toward Allison's door.

"I guess he knew about me?" Delia asked.

"He figured it out last summer, though I never admitted to anything." Paul chuckled. "When I had breakfast with him last week at the Wagon Wheel, he asked if I was dating. I told him there was someone I was talking to, but I hadn't seen her in a while."

A quick gust of summer wind breezed by, lifting Delia's hair slightly off her shoulder. Meeting her eyes, he reached toward her face, taking a strand of hair, and tucking it behind her ear. His fingers traced her jawbone down to her chin. "I see you are growing your hair out again. I like it longer."

"Father Wainwright! Are you still a priest?" Delia drawled, batting her eyelashes. She flattened her hand to her heart. "Are you flirting with me?"

He nuzzled her neck. "Mmm . . . I hope so. Not sure I know how to flirt anymore."

She fanned herself, "I assure you, you're doing fine."

"And yes, I'm still a priest until my paperwork goes through. The bishop is saying probably by December."

"What if it doesn't?"

Paul grabbed Delia's hand, enjoying the energy radiating between them. "Well, if you truly want to know, I'm not going back. Even if I'm denied laicization, I will just be done. Like quitting my job. But my paid administrative leave is up at the end of the year, so after that, I'll need to find some way to support myself."

"Are you working a lot now?"

"I volunteer as my nephews' basketball coach. But for work right now it's just as the Monday night facilitator with the Stolen Voices group. I'm loving that role. It's only a couple of hours a week, but it is really rewarding. I honestly feel like I'm making more of a difference there than I ever did as a priest. Maybe this is where God wants me to be."

"I'm glad you got in with them."

"How about you?"

"Gotta tell you, that was a wonderful idea you gave me. Into the Light is a great organization. I've been speaking at high schools. I've even been invited to talk at a conference in Houston next month about how I was groomed." Delia shuddered. "You'd be shocked at the number of teenagers—girls and boys—who have been approached by sex traffickers. After an assembly last week, I met with these three girls who were about fifteen . . ." She shook her head. "I got them in touch with a couple of FBI agents who handle the worst of humanity. Those girls believed they would be starting their acting career in Vegas this weekend. They had no idea what they were in for. They thought they were being approached by a talent agent who promised them a chance to go into show business."

"I'm impressed you've been able to take your past and find a way to save souls!" Paul said. "I really admire how you've found a way to turn your experience into something positive. Looks like you've found your calling."

"I think so. I want some good to come out of my time at the Dragon." She placed her hand on Paul's shoulder. "I was a bit nervous about coming today. I wasn't sure you could ever forgive me . . ."

"I forgave you long ago." Paul squeezed her hand. "Have you forgiven me?"

"Forgiven and forgotten."

"Uncle Paul!" Garret and Archie flew out the front door, speeding down the stone path. "Mom said you've got to bring your friend inside *this minute*," Archie said, his middle two teeth missing.

"Did she now?" Delia chuckled, bending down. "You must be Garret. And you must be Archie."

"Tell your mom I said she's bossy and we will be in shortly."

"Uncle Paul," Garret sighed. "You know she'll get grumpy if I tell her you said that."

"Well, then tell her I said she cannot be angry at you for repeating the truth."

"Oh okay!" Garret brightened at his uncle's logic.

"Nice to meet you!" Archie called over his shoulder as the boys ran back inside.

From the sidewalk, Paul heard, "Mommm, Uncle Paul says you're bossy and you can't get mad when I tell you the truth!"

"You're in for it now," Delia laughed.

"I was going to say the same for you. Are you sure you are ready for this?"

"Just a second, I have something for you." She opened the Camry's back door. "Happy birthday," Delia said, thrusting the bag at Paul. He gave her a questioning look. "Oh, come on! You said this was a birthday party for your sister. Did you forget you told me you're twins? Open it!"

Paul pushed away the tissue paper, discovering a gold name placard. It read, "Paul Wainwright."

"For your desk. When do you start at the University of Texas?"

"Delia, thank you." He ran his hands across the engraved letters. "In August. I just found out they added a second Intro to Psychology class to my courses, so I have those plus I'm teaching one Comparative Religions class. It's part-time. But I'll be here in Tyler, near my family."

Paul's voice changed as he rocked back on his heels. "I'm so glad you came. I know I haven't seen you in months and maybe I'm rushing things, but I'm going to throw it out there anyway." He reached for her hand. "I'd like to talk about starting again. You and me—with plans toward a future. If you don't mind something long-distance for now, maybe I can look at moving to Shreveport when the fall semester is finished."

Delia smiled. "Actually, I wanted to talk with you." She took a long inhale. "Ginny owns Saint George's. As you are aware, the Diocese of Tyler is as large as the country of Ireland. They are our biggest customer. She's been wanting to open a location here for quite a while. She found a spot near the Cathedral and is planning on opening a second store in September. I could transfer here and run the new shop. She's offered me the position."

"What about your mom? You'd be far from her."

"Maddy just graduated and took that job in Oklahoma City. She convinced Mama to move there with her. I'm glad too. She'll get a real house for the first time, not the rundown shack we grew up in. Tommy is helping her move in two weeks."

"Really? You'd come to Tyler?"

"Look, Paul, it's the first time we've seen each other since January. I don't want to put any pressure on you . . ."

Paul slipped his arm around her waist. "You aren't. Are you kidding? God is good. So are you. I love the idea. You know I wouldn't invite you today just so you could be hazed by my brother and sister unless I wanted to see if we could make this work, right?" Leaning over, he cupped her chin and planted a soft kiss on her lips.

"Oh my! Mr. Wainwright," Delia gasped, right as Paul leaned in for another.

"Mom! Uncle Paul is kissing his friend!" came a report from inside.

"You ready to meet the crazy?" Paul whispered as they broke apart.

Delia took his hand. "You bet. Let's do this."

Acknowledgements

G RATITUDE IS MY LOVE language. Every draft of this book was shaped, developed and created with the help of several loving souls to whom I owe a great deal of appreciation. Ginny Humber, Ana Christina Jarrin, Sheryl Soffer, Susan Mills offered me patience, advice, and feedback. Many friends listened to my story, encouraged me and read chapters, passages or even the entire manuscript at one time or another. To them, I am much obliged.

Additionally, I am beyond grateful and sincerely humbled by the following professionals who helped me polish this novel. Maricel Gasga provided developmental edits. Sarah Lubratt line edited my story and pointed out a significant flaw in an earlier draft of my story. Bethany Dancel, of Dancel Editorial LLC, proofread and offered me words of encouragement she didn't know I needed at that exact moment. And a special thank you to Karen Lewis, of Simply Amusing Designs, for her amazing cover art and putting up with my creative flightiness.

A special thank you goes out to my family who listened to countless hours of storyline, edits and rewrites, and especially my husband who helped me understand how a man would react to certain points of views. I am blessed beyond measure.

About the Author

Elaina Harper lives in East Texas with her husband and two children. She's the Emotional Support Human, to Luna the dog. She won her first writing contest at the age of six. When she isn't writing, she's playing in her garden, watching the Arizona Diamondbacks, or has her nose in a book.

If you enjoyed reading this, please leave a review on Amazon. I read every review. Plus, they help new readers discover my books. Thank you.